The Lightest, Heaviest Things

To Dr. Betty, because she said so. And to Katie Grace, because she said not to.

--W.P.--

I.

The trees are tall, and the giants are not actually taller than the trees. You told me the giants aren't real. I don't know if they're real. They look real, to me, but they also don't seem real. You don't see them, either.

"Wink?" I call, standing in the clearing. "Wink?"

The pink and purple pine needles are slippy beneath my bare feet, as I turn in a circle. I call for her again, but she's not here. That's okay, I decide. She's not here *yet*. She will be here. Eventually.

I wiggle my toes, but pine needles aren't like grass. They don't tickle your bare feet. They poke, and they prick. It's a very unpleasant feeling--almost as unpleasant as being without Wink. Pine needles are dead and dry. There is nothing interesting about them, and there is nothing interesting about being without Wink.

"Wink?" I call one more time hopefully.

I don't hear Wink, but I do hear the giant.

I hear the giant's footsteps before he approaches me. The ground doesn't shake beneath him, for although the giants sound heavy, they are the lightest beings I know.

He looks at me with deep sad eyes. Orange like dying embers. He sits in front of me, pulling his knees up to his chest; mimicking me. I laugh.

The giants never laugh.

Not hearing Wink approach, I startle as she sits down. "Hi, Peri!" she says, cheerfully. She holds her hand out. "Sorry, it took awhile for the paint to dry."

Wink has one long pinkie nail on her left hand. It's the one nail she paints, and she does tiny, elaborate designs. Today it's golden mountain majesty, even more impressive than last week's purple.

"Nice," I murmur. My eyes flicker back up to the giant.

He just looks at me. He doesn't speak. He's sad.

"Come on," Wink says, standing, then grabbing my arm and suddenly yanking me to my feet. "Let's go!"

I'm slow and listless as she drags me through the trees because I can feel the giant's presence looming behind me although he doesn't follow. Or is he ahead?

There's a chirping noise "Do you hear that?" Wink asks.

I nod.

"Do you know what it is?"

I shake my head.

"It's a tree frog!" She beams. "I had to write a paper on tree frogs." She holds up her fingernail again. "Maybe I should do a tree frog next time." She grins at me. "What do you think?"

"I *like* frogs," I say. Then I swear I can feel the breath of a giant--but Wink would say that's just the wind.

It's different, though.

As we continue walking, Wink points out a few more animal sounds, telling me what they are.

Then I stumble to the ground and Wink blinks at me in surprise. Anxiously, "Peri? Did you… did you fall?"

I'd prefer not to answer that question. I cross my eyes and focus on the little rocks in front of me. "Look!" I say. "These rocks are sparkly."

Wink dives down laying flat on the ground next to me. She crosses her eyes to look at the rocks, too. "Magic," she breathes.

Wink believes in everyday magic.

Wink does not believe in the giants.

But today she stands up, pulling me to my feet again. Then she picks a rock up off the ground and presses it into my hand. "For protecting you."

"For… for protecting me from what?" I turn it over in my hands.

She blinks at me seriously. "From the giants." She shoves her hands in her pockets and doesn't want to talk about it anymore. But I realize that, for the first time, maybe she's seen one.

"I know they look scary," I say, holding the rock up to the light gazing at the sparkles. "But they're really just sad. And scared."

"What are they scared of, Peri?" she asks.

"I don't know."

"Are they going to follow me, now, like they follow you?"

Tucking the rock in my pocket, I choose one from the ground and hand it to Wink. "Maybe we can help them find out what they're scared of. And save them."

Wink closes her eyes. "Yeah."

I grab her arm. "Maybe with both of us seeing them, we can get them to talk!"

"Maybe they don't talk," she says, thoughtfully.

Then, in unplanned unison, we say, "Maybe they communicate some other way."

And we will figure it out.

II.

Sitting on the floor of my room, I watch my pale purple curtains dance, tousled by the wind through the open window. I worry about Wink. It's been two days and I haven't heard from her.

In my peripheral vision, through the window and down in my yard, I see a giant. He's sitting on the dried, end-of-summer grass, his knees pulled up to his chest. Just like me.

I wonder if one is watching Wink right now.

I wonder how hers sits.

Maybe it sits criss-cross applesauce like she does.

I run my fingers over the worn wooden planks of my floor, letting my fingertips linger on the cracks. I think about all of the dust that shifts through this floor to the downstairs, and I wonder if anyone else thinks about the dust. I bet Wink thinks about the dust. I should ask sometime.

I glance back out the window, and my eyes meet a pair of huge, dying-ember ones. I feel a wave of sadness for the giants, and I tear my eyes away.

I curl up on the floor watching a minuscule spider scuttle past my face. Its tiny, pale green legs move in clumsy tandem as he runs from foes unknown to me. Yawning, I close my eyes, letting my lashes rest upon my cheeks. Before I realize that I'm tired, I'm peacefully asleep.

Do the giants sleep? I've only ever seen them awake and staring sadly. Furthermore, they are always alone. The only way I know there's more than one is by the feelings, those overhanging feelings I get when a giant is nearby. They're slightly different at times, and they just feel like different people. I guess I can't explain it. I just know.

I wake up hours later with the light of an orange-red sunset flooding the room. The phone is ringing and that is what has awakened me. I yawn, stretch, and glance out the window.

The giant is gone.

I wonder what he's feeling.

Where do they go?

I clamber down the stairs to the phone on the wall. I answer it, feeling slightly nervous "Hello?"

"Peri!"

It's Wink.

I am at ease. "Oh, Wink, it's you."

"You're home alone again," she says. It's not a question. Sometimes we both just know things. I nod, then remember I'm on the phone. "Yes," I say, softly. I trace my finger along the spiraling gray flowers on the faded wallpaper. I hear her sigh. I lean against the wall.

"I'll be right over," she says after I've begun to wonder if she's hung up. "Okay?"

She hangs up before I can say okay.

I go out and sit on the porch steps. Before I know it, I'm crying. I'm not sure why. I'm still crying when Wink arrives, all clatter and growl on her parents' dilapidated tractor. She parks it, turns it off, and comes running to hug me. "Peri," she whispers, "Peri, it's okay."

I wait for her to explain why she didn't call for three days; why my life was so unbearably still and quiet for three days. She just hugs me, and I find myself being angry with her. Then I hug her back tightly and cry harder because at that moment, I'm really not angry at all.

"Peri," she whispers, "we're going to save the giants." She pulls away and places her hands on my shoulder, her gray eyes shining. "We are meant to save them."

"How do you know?"

She jumps up. "Just like I know when it's going to rain, or I know that we're best friends, or I know my next sibling's going to be a boy," she declares. "I just feel it."

I stand up. "I know what you mean!"

Sometimes we both just know things.

We glance around.

"I don't see any," we whisper at the same time.

The giants are real, but sometimes we don't know where they go. Sometimes that scares us, but you don't seem nearly as scared as me. I don't know if you're faking courage. But maybe I'm faking a little bit of fear, so... it is what it is.

III.

I don't know if there are others like us. I wonder why I can't remember the first time I saw the giants. I wonder why you never saw them before now. You do really see them, right?

Wink and I have been making small talk for hours, and then she drops the question on me.

"Peri? Where'd your parents go this time?"

I glance at the floor, and then I look back up at her. "Tibet," I say softly. "An opportunity came up."

She purses her lips. "Did they say when they'd be back?"

I shake my head.

She sighs. "You'll be okay," she tells me firmly.

I don't *want* to be okay and I don't *want* to be alone with the giants anymore, particularly now that she can see them too. I hope that she'll ask me to come stay with her and her crazy family, but she doesn't and I would never ask.

We're in my kitchen now. We've been sitting at the big white table on the sleek black-stained wooden stools that don't match the rest of the house. My parents brought those back from their last trip. There's a sudden lull in the conversation, and I think I can feel a giant--maybe. It's faint.

I glance out the window.

There, sitting by Wink's tractor, is a giant.

"Wink," I whisper. "Look."

She glances around. "What?"

I point out the window.

"Oh," she says, softly. "Oh, look at him."

"You really see him?" I ask. I'm terrified that she's lying to me, though I really don't know why.

"Of course I see him! Look at his sad orange eyes."

I never told her their eyes were orange, and she's looking directly at him.

Of *course* she's telling me the truth!

We watch the giant get up slowly, clumsily, and lumber off into the surrounding forest. He ducks into the pink and purple pine trees and it's like he was never there.

We gaze out the window in silence for what feels like forever; then Wink pokes me with her long pinkie nail. I glance down.

She's painted it gray with a little green tree frog peeking above her cuticle to look at me in surprise.

I giggle. "Tree frogs," I say.

She nods. She beams. "Tree frogs."

IV.

The next morning, Wink and I wake up at the same time, even though there's barely any daylight yet. We yawn and lie there side-by-side in our blanket fort knowing there are giants nearby.

"It's weird," she whispers finally. "I see one giant when I'm away from you and you see one giant then too. But when we're together, we just see the one. Not two."

I lean my head on her shoulder, except her shoulder is poky and knobby; so I shift again, snuggling back into the pillows on my side of the pallet. I press my cheek against the light cotton and breathe in the smell of the fabric softener I used the last time I washed sheets. "They only ever appear alone," I whisper. "There's one in particular that usually comes to me, but sometimes there are others."

"I've only seen one, except for the ones with you," she whispers. "I haven't seen mine since I left home yesterday."

We wonder why.

"Maybe giants can't be together," she suggests. Then she gasps. "Maybe it's a *curse.*"

I bet she's right! After all, if there's everyday magic and giants and sparkling magic rocks and our just knowing things, then curses might exist too.

We get up and take down the fort, although neither of us really decides to or says that we should. We're nearly done, the pillows are back on the bed, and I'm fluffing them when she says, "Hey, Peri? I'm sorry I never believed you about the giants."

I elbow her. *"I almost didn't believe me about the giants."*

She smacks me with a pillow and I collapse onto the bed in giggles.

She places her finger on my lips. "Shh," she says. "This is serious." But her mouth turns up at the corners.

I do calm after a while and she perches on the bed next to me. "We need to research the giants," she says.

I don't know why we always whisper when we're in my house. Maybe because it's such a lonely building and we're afraid to disturb the isolation.

"Maybe your mom could help us," I suggest hopefully. I like her mom; her mom smells like cookies and oatmeal. Her mom is warm and clever and always seems to know exactly how to help.

She shakes her head quickly, and then I catch her glaring at me for a second before she smooths her features over again. I think that I could cry, if I'd let myself; I think that I could let myself, if she weren't here. "No," she says, and I don't know if I'm imagining the new harsh edge to her voice or if it's really there. "We can do it on our own."

I nod quickly, still holding back my tears, questioning my perception. I never understand how we can go from giggling to not-quite-fighting so quickly. I don't mean for it to happen. Of course, Wink probably doesn't mean for it to happen either.

Sometimes, when things don't make sense, I'm so tempted to just blame the giants. I glance out my window, but there is no giant there.

Wink pokes me. "Hey," she says, softly, "we'll figure it out." She fidgets a bit. "Want to go to the library with me tomorrow? Grandpa's driving into town, and he said he'd drop me off at the library. We could look for something on giants, or curses, or magic in general."

I nod a tiny little jerk of my head.

She stands up and nods decisively. "See you tomorrow then!"

"You're leaving?" I try to keep my voice from squeaking. She cocks her head, and then nods, edging towards my doorway.

"Mom will need me," she says. "You understand."

I nod and let her go even though I don't understand, because no one ever needs me.

It's not until later that day when I am eating my lunch, surrounded by quiet, that it occurs to me that *maybe the giants do.*

Maybe everyone needs everyone all of the time, or maybe no one needs anyone. Maybe it doesn't matter. And maybe I'll never know. Or maybe the giants will tell me.

V.

I am always alone, except I never am because of the giants. They're not my preferred companions. I'd much rather be surrounded by noise, by color, by adventure. Instead I have been handed solemn, sad, quiet. I can't figure out what to do with it.

Wink's grandfather drops us off at the street corner, a little ways away from the library. He grins widely at us. "Enjoy your independence, girls," he tells us, as we realize that we will be walking by ourselves for a little bit. Living in the country makes town seem scary and exciting. My heart hammers in my chest, and I so badly want to ask him to walk with us; but he is already driving away and Wink is beaming and grabbing my hand and dragging me down the street. I forget to worry because the sunshine is warm on my face. I smile up at the sky, squinting my eyes shut--like I'm thanking the sun. If there are magic rocks and giants and curses, and if Wink and I can just know things, then the sun can feel my thank-yous; and maybe that makes it warmer.

Sometimes I think I'm in love with *maybe.*

Like how *maybe* we'll save the giants.

Wink spins a bit when we enter the library and taps the toes of her sneakers together. "Do you feel it?" she asks.

I just feel the quiet, which is nothing different from my every day. I cock my head.

"The quiet," she says. "You don't get that every day."

Maybe she doesn't. I do. I hate it. I hate it as much as I hate the fact that she doesn't realize that I do.

Wink stacks up books--many books--fairytales, picture books, and even books from the adult section. I raise my eyebrows at her and then push those last ones away.

"Those won't help," I guarantee her. She agrees, I can tell. Sometimes we both just know things. She nods decisively like she does, and she picks up a book.

She is instantly submerged in another world.

She spends the rest of the afternoon reading, but I don't. I wander around, hum under my breath, and wish I could run back outside into the smiling sun away from all of this quiet.

Sometimes when I'm at home, I feel like this too. Like I should run away as far as I can, the way my parents always do (Greece, Russia, Djibouti, Tibet). Then I wonder why they don't take me with them. Then I wonder why the giants stay here in the rare pink-and-purple pine trees. They should run away as far as they can.

Maybe they will after Wink and I save them.

Maybe they'll take me with them.

Sometimes I dream that I am flying, flying away. I leave home behind me. I fly very far, and I find my parents. When I try to land with them, though, I am blown away. It is only then that I realize that, when I left home behind me, I also left Wink. I wake up scared.

VI.

When Wink finds what she's looking for, I think the whole library knows. She shoves a book into my arms, her eyes sparkling, and she points at a page. "I've found it," she whispers. "It's really beginning."

Oh my goodness, I think, *it's really beginning!*

We sit on the floor of the library; she's criss-cross-applesauce, and I am curled up like a cat. We read the story together. It's a single page, hidden in a book of children's stories; it is yellowed and a bit ragged looking. It's about giants--a city of giants, far away in a land where the clouds hang low and the mountains reach high and the rivers gush, crystal-clear. The giants in the city fight each other, and lie to each other, and hurt each other--until one day a satyress comes down from her hidden mountain cave. She holds out her ancient staff and curses them--if they cannot work together, then they shall be alone. That is how it ends

Wink and I both cry, although neither of us is quite comfortable with the other knowing that. Then we go to the front desk, and check the book out--I use my mom's card. After all, it's not like she'll be using it anytime soon.

"Peri," Wink whispers to me as we leave the building after her grandfather has come in to get us. "Peri, we have to undo the curse. We have to help the giants because being alone is *bad.*"

"I know," I say. I want to add, *I know it even better than you do;* but I know I'll feel bad about that later, so I don't. Instead I nudge her with my shoulder. "What do you think happened to that satyress?"

Wink doesn't answer until we are in the back seat of her grandfather's pickup truck, buckling our seatbelts. Then she speaks, leaning close to me. I can hear her, but her grandfather can't hear her over the country song blaring through the radio. "I don't know, but I do wonder what happened to her. Why she never returned the giants to their home. How we can return them now."

I sniffle a bit, but I don't cry now. "Maybe we need her staff."

Wink gasps. "Of *course,* Peri! I bet she hid it somewhere clever, knowing we would come along and need it to save the giants!"

I know she is right, and she knows it, too. Sometimes we both just know things.

We stare down at the book, feeling a sudden weight of responsibility upon our shoulders. How can we save the giants?

How can we find the staff?

How can we both just know things?

We will figure it out.

The giants are not in town; they are only in the quiet, lonely woods. Maybe they can't bear to go into town and see all of the people hugging and waving and talking. Maybe it hurts their hearts so much that they just run away to the woods and sit and feel sad. Maybe after we save them, they can run to their homes and to their families and to their friends. Maybe it will be a hundred times warmer than a smile at the sun. And maybe I'm in love with the maybes.

VII.

I am always waiting, always hoping, to be anywhere, anywhere but here. Yet, here I remain.

I sit at the foot of the stairs, my back against the wall. The telephone hangs above my head, still and quiet. I wait.

It doesn't ring.

Wink promised that she'd call but that doesn't mean she will. She often can't; she's helping her mom or her grandfather. They need her so much.

Goodness, how I wish I were needed.

I can't sit here anymore; I can't keep waiting, drowning in the deep gray loneliness.

If she calls, then I'll miss the call, I decide. And she can just wonder why.

My passive-aggressive course of action determined, I run outside and into the cold. The screen door slams behind me, calling a lonely call that will never be answered—for what could answer it?

I run, barefoot feet slapping the dusty ground, face turned towards the cold, unwelcoming sun. Finally, I stop at the edge of the driveway, glancing over my shoulder.

A giant stands by the house, blinking tear-filled, bright orange eyes at me. He shifts his weight from one massive foot to the other. He rubs his eyes with his huge, pale hands.

I wonder--does he think I'm leaving him? I turn all the way around to face him. "I'm not leaving," I call shakily. "I'm still going to help you. I just…" I don't even know if he understands English. I hug my own shoulders, shivering a bit. It's not that cold outside--but I feel cold inside. And I think the giant understands that. I think he also wonders how it can be really beginning, yet be this still and quiet. If it were really beginning… wouldn't Wink be here?

Of course, the giants came to me first.

I realize this suddenly.

The giants came to me first, and I didn't even think to help them until Wink came. I realize that I can interpret that two ways-- Either, obviously I need her--or… Obviously, obviously I don't.

I realize, now, that I wait for Wink too much. This is a shocking concept. I sit down on the ground and stare at the giant. He sits, too, and I feel the ground shake just the slightest bit--The giants are the lightest,heaviest things.

We contemplate ourselves, the giant and I.

Who is he?

He is the first giant, the one that came to me so many summers ago--with his thick, dark hair and sad, orange eyes. He is my particular giant, this first one.

Who am I?

I am Peri Milligan, and I wish I were anywhere but right here. I always, always wish that I were anywhere but here.

So… why do I stay here, always, always?

Why do I wait for someone else to save me?

For someone else to save the giants?

For Wink to call me?

And in that moment, I think, maybe I feel a little lighter. Like maybe I am also one of the lightest, heaviest things.

I'm going to find the staff of the satyress.

I'm going to save the giants.

VIII.

The giants are always, always near me--even when I can't feel them or see them. It's like by being as close to others as they can sometimes, the giants feel better about having to be alone the rest of the time. I have to wonder, though--late at night, when it's all over and they can hear themselves existing again, doesn't it hurt all the more because of the glimpses of togetherness?

It's a long walk to Wink's house, but I go anyway. I put on my high-tops, I pull back my hair, and I go anyway. There is a giant following me, somewhere behind. It is interesting to me how the giants always hang back, staying a little behind. Sometimes, I can feel them when they're *just* out of view.

The giants are good at hiding.

I'd like to whistle as I walk, but something in me won't let me. Something in me says that this is very solemn. That I should be very careful. That I need to stay alert and be prepared for anything. Maybe that's how you know that it's really beginning--you can feel everything changing, a little bit.

The pine trees lean against each other, whispering. Maybe they're saying, *it's-beginning, it's-beginning, it's-beginning.* Or maybe they're saying, *be-careful, be-careful, be-careful.*

When I finally reach Wink's house, I stop in the driveway to take in the rambling, faded yellow farmhouse. I can already feel the energy coming from inside and hear the giggling shrieks of Wink's younger siblings who seem to be perpetually caught up in a game of tag. I just soak it in for a second--the glorious sound.

Then I approach the front door.

Before I can knock, Wink throws it open. "Peri! I knew you'd come."

On the one hand, I am sad--I have not surprised her. On the other hand, sometimes we both just know things--and maybe that's our brand of magic.

Deciding between sadness and happiness is surprisingly difficult. Finally, I decide to smile. "Hi, Wink." I shift my weight. I find myself searching my senses for the presence of giants, but I can't feel them now. I wonder what they're up to. I know they're still there, somewhere.

"What's up?" she asks, opening the door further to let me in.

I so badly want to go in.

But I came here with a mission and going inside derails that.

If I go in, then I will want to stay.

"I want to go looking for the satyress," I whisper--but it's a decisive whisper. It's a whisper that she can't argue with.

"Oh," she says, and now she seems surprised. "Oh, um..." she glances at her sandal-clad feet. "I'm not sure we're nearly prepared enough, and--"

I shush her. "Can't you hear it?" I whisper. "Can't you hear it in the trees?"

We both hold our breath, and I swear her siblings quiet down, too.

It's-beginning, it's-beginning, it's-beginning.

Be-careful, be-careful, be-careful.

"I do hear it," she says.

"Then come on," I say, stepping back. I am impatient. I don't want to go without her, but I just might. I am feeling unpredictable. I am feeling dangerous. I am not feeling like myself, exactly.

She says nothing.

I take another step back.

"Let me change shoes," she says suddenly. "Then, yes, let's go."

It's beginning, and we must be careful. What are we being careful of? It's easier to be careful, when you know what to be careful of. Otherwise, you're crashing through the forest blind and in the dark.

IX.

This may sound strange, but my plan is just to walk through the forest until I get somewhere. I figure I'll know where somewhere is when we get there. I feel like we should head north, maybe--thus, that's where I lead Wink, and I'm revelling in the leading. It isn't often that I am the one doing the leading; Wink usually does that.

I am surprised that she is letting me--it's unlike her.

However, after we have been walking through the forest for about ten minutes, Wink finally does voice concerns.

"Why are we going north?"

Why shouldn't we go north, I wonder. *Doesn't the north feel right?*

"Peri?"

I stop walking, and I shrug before crossing my arms. "Which direction do you want to go?" I demand. I'm being moody, and I know it.

Wink's eyes go wide. "Peri, I don't care which direction we go, as long as it's the right direction."

I don't know what the right direction is, but I don't want to admit that--I'm supposed to be the leader this time. I just glare at the ground.

"Peri?" Her voice hitches. "Peri, if we aren't really doing this, then I need to go home."

"You always need to go home," I mutter.

"What's that supposed to mean?"

I'm not sure, and I don't actually want to figure it out either. I glare at a fallen log just a few inches from my feet. A bright red ladybug skitters across the moss, disappearing into a crevice. I wish that I could disappear, too.

"Well?" Wink says, demanding that I look back up at her. Our eyes meet, and for a moment, I think we're challenging each other.

The moment is broken by a strange voice, soft as moss and hard as rock.

"Disrupting the quiet in the loudest way… what are you doing in the forest today?"

Wink and I jump, and somehow wind up standing closer together, our teeth chattering. Suddenly, the world feels much colder.

We turn around and are faced with a person who seems to have appeared out of the very air of the forest. On first glance, we identify him as being both more and less human than ourselves-- and I think that's why we don't run. We can't; we are too curious. After all, how could we not be--a boy with dark silver skin is looking at us with huge eyes that are of a much paler silver. He blinks, and then says again, "What are you doing in the forest today?"

"What *are* you?"

There's a pause, and it takes me a beat to realize that I am the one that has spoken. Before I can feel actual proper shame, however, the boy is speaking again.

"I'm a lot of things, actually—but you wouldn't believe me if I told you factually."

Wink and I exchange confused glances, then look back at the boy.

He's blushing a silvery blush. "I'm not actually supposed to have spoken to you," he admits. "So now I don't know what to do." He rubs the back of his neck.

We wait.

"I'm a troll," he admits. "Like a bridge troll. We control the bridges between worlds."

"You *what?*" Wink and I gasp in unison—actually, we might have accidentally harmonized.

He starts to step back into the forest. "Well," he says. He doesn't seem to know how to continue.

"That's amazing," I say, stepping towards him. "That's amazing." *Giants and trolls.*

"I'm a troll," he repeats in a whisper. "My name is Ull."

I hold out my hand for him to shake. "Hello, Ull."

He looks at my hand confusedly, but then he smiles. "I like your hands," he says, quietly.

I draw back my hand nervously and slip it in my pocket. He smiles at me, then turns to Wink to inspect her hands. He taps the pinkie nail. "Long," he says. "Long and... colorful?" He looks at the other nails, unpainted and short. He shrugs. "I like it very much."

Then he pulls away, leaving us exchanging confused and uncomfortable glances.

"Humans have lovely, but dangerous hands," he says, getting a faraway look in his eyes. "Hands that have shaped the earth, moving its mountains and digging in its sands. That's what my father always says."

Wink and I exchange glances. "So you know about humans?" Wink says, cocking her head. "Because we don't know about trolls. Or, we didn't until just now."

He nods, closing his eyes and swaying back and forth a bit, like a tree stirred by the wind--but there is no wind. It is like he is thinking of a wind that isn't there.

"We're trespassers in your world," he says. "My family is. But, you have known of us... or, of things we do." He gestures to the trees. "The pink-and-purple pines are ours, though you've assumed that they belong to you."

Wink and I gasp--for, of course, that explains the question that the entire town of Valley Low has been asking for twenty years--*where did the pink-and-purple pine trees come from?*

I shiver, for I feel that whisper again. *It's-beginning, it's-beginning, it's-beginning.*

"It was scary when the scientists came," he says. "We hadn't been expecting that, and we had to hide. Well, my parents had to--they went in the mountain, tucked away inside. I wasn't born yet; the world was not yet familiar with my name."

"How do you know English?" I ask, looking into his silvery eyes. He furrows his brow.

"Is *that* what I'm speaking?" he demands. "I knew it was a harder one." When he sees confusion written on our faces, he explains. "Sorry, yes. Trolls can speak all tongues of all worlds naturally--but some are harder." He laughs. "I've always heard that English is difficult because it has more exceptions to the rules than not."

Wink and I giggle, nodding. We have often comisserated the unique difficulties of our language.

"Do trolls have their own language?" I ask--it seems the obvious next question.

He nods, his eyes lighting up. "Trollish, I suppose, is what you would call it, in your own words... Though, we call it many things. The sounds of the mountains when they sigh, and of the birds when they softly sing."

"Can you speak some?" Wink asks, enamored with this description.

He smiles even more widely. "You have already heard it in my name. I am Ull, but our word for *return* is quite the same."

"Return," I repeat.

It's-beginning, it's-beginning, it's-beginning.

He nods.

"Return," he whispers, and once again he sways as though moved by a wind that only he can feel.

X.

Ull is very odd, and maybe that's why we like him. It's easy to like people who don't care if you like them or not, and who also seem to like you. There are no uncomfortable expectations that way.

He wants to take us to meet his parents—this makes me and Wink very nervous. We aren't sure how we feel about meeting grown-up trolls. We don't know how they feel about trespassers, especially human trespassers. We are especially worried, since Ull tells us he isn't even supposed to have talked to us, let alone to have invited us to lunch.

"I don't know," I say. "Will your parents appreciate that?"

He smiles a soft smile. "Actually," he says, quietly, "they might be expecting you."

We're not sure what to make of that, but we feel oddly reassured--or, at least I do. I think Wink must, too, because we both follow him deeper into the woods. If Wink is still wanting to go home, she doesn't say so.

He leads us farther from home than we've ever been before. We've been walking for quite some time when it occurs to me that we are actually going up the mountain. I feel a shiver of excitement up my spine and through my shoulder blades. I've never gone up the mountain. The old folks of Valley Low say that odd things happen to those who go up the mountain.

I guess they're right.

It gets quieter the further up we go. I'm just beginning to think that we will never get there when Ull pauses. "This is it," he says. He breaks the silence abruptly and Wink jumps a bit. We both feel as though we had begun to fall asleep but have now been forcibly awakened.

It doesn't look like 'it,' if you know what I mean. We are standing in a small cluster of pink-and-purple pines which are surrounded by an encroaching army of deep green spruce. The ground is slick with dried needles and the sky has turned moody and gray.

I often feel like that sky.

Ull clears his throat and speaks softly. He must be speaking in Trollish, for it is far too beautiful for me to understand. I promise that the breeze carries his words away gently, cradling them and caressing them.

Slowly, the ground seems to open up--I really don't have a better way of describing it. The ground parts, and pine needles are slipping, slipping--

I blink, and there are stairs leading down into the ground.

"Come on," Ull says, heading down the stairs.

Wink and I exchange glances.

"This is very exciting," she says, smiling.

I nod. It *is*. It's the most exciting thing that has ever happened to me. This is the farthest from home I've ever been. This is the strangest set of circumstances I've ever been in.

For the first time in my life, though, a little bit of my soul feels like maybe it's right at home. Right at home and finding more home every moment.

We follow him down the earthen stairs and into the ground.

Finally, Ull stops. As we reach him, we realize that we must have finally made it to the house--well, *home* is probably a better word. For we have come to a landing which broadens out into a large, round room--and it's surprisingly well-lit for being a hole in the ground.

Ull calls. It's a soft, wild sound--like a bird singing after an early morning rain. He blushes a silvery blush when he catches me and Wink watching him. Like he's just done something very personal and he'd forgotten that we were there.

A warbling, comforting sound replies from somewhere deeper within the cavern. I see Ull's dark silver lips twitch in a smile. "Mom," he says, happily, when a lady troll emerges from the shadows.

She looks a lot like him, except a much paler, greener silver. She's quite lovely, with fluffy silver hair framing her small pointy face. She looks comforting, but not--a bit like Wink's mom, but a bit ethereal, too. She seems to be thinking of other places far, far away. Like Ull seems to when he's swaying. She doesn't seem surprised to see me and Wink standing there awkwardly in our scuffed shoes and baggy t-shirts--I can't help but realize that Ull and his mom are dressed in clothes that look homespun, probably from some sort of plant fiber.

She smiles at us, and beckons us nearer. "Hello," she says, softly. "I figured it wouldn't be long, now--although, I wasn't expecting the two of you to be so young." Her eyes look happy and sad at the same time. I know that feeling very well.

Another troll enters now and I realize that Ull must take after his father. Their faces are more rectangular than Ull's mother's face--her face makes me think of triangles. As the light catches the dark silver skin and lips of both father and son, their light silver eyes contrast beautifully. They are iridescent.

"Hello," Ull's father says in a voice that comes from somewhere deeper than the ocean. "Hello." He seems surprised--not that we are there, but that we are ourselves.

Wink and I don't know what to say. I don't mean to stare, but I do. It's okay, I find--the adult trolls are staring at us, too. Ull sways as he hums. Something about the way he does that makes me think that maybe he does it all the time. That it's like having a heartbeat or breathing. He hums. He breathes. He sways. He lives.

The silence has only just begun to feel uncomfortable instead of reverent when Ull's father clears his throat. "It's beginning," he says.

That's what I've been hearing, part of me wants to scream.

It's-beginning, it's-beginning, it's-beginning.

Maybe my face gives away my internal battle to stay quiet because Ull's mother smiles at me and steps over to place her hands on my cheeks. Her palms are warm--I hadn't realized how cold I was until then. I shiver and blink at her, looking into her deep green eyes.

"You can scream, you know," she whispers. She whispers it so low that I'm not sure that Wink or Ull hear it. It's like it reverberates through my chest and into my core.

I don't know what it means and I probably look stupid trying to figure it out. She steps away and I look at the ground, frustrated with myself.

"It's beginning," the father troll says again. And he turns to Ull. "Return."

Ull hums a little louder, swaying and swaying and swaying.

XI.

"What's beginning?" Wink asks. "Can you tell me?"

She turns to me and I see frustration glint in her eyes. We are sitting at an old wooden table in another room of the trolls' house. I have been agreeing with them--that it clearly is beginning. I haven't realized how quiet Wink has been until she speaks. I have the sudden sinking realization that I haven't been looking out for her. I should have been--she would have noticed my silence and been there for me. Right? She would've…

"You remember," I say, "you were the first to say it was really beginning. When we were in the library."

She is stone-faced. "Okay," she says. I raise my eyebrows, but she looks at the ground.

I glance at Ull, wishing he weren't seeing this. I wish Wink and I were a unified front. We're supposed to be best friends-- shouldn't we act like it?

"We're going to save the giants," I remind her. Why, oh why can't we both just know things, right now? "We're going to figure it out." I glance at Mr. Troll--I'm not sure what to call him, so this is what I've settled on. "Right?"

"Of course you are, girls," he says. He turns his gaze towards Ull. "The return is beginning."

I want to take Wink's hand and squeeze it and remind her that we're in this together. I'd like to apologize to her, and plead for her to be---but what, I don't know. I don't take her hand. I just look at it. At her pinkie nail, painted bright orange and tipped with dark blue. Orange like the giants' eyes. Blue like I don't know what.

She has fallen silent again.

I want to get up, run, cry, but of course I don't.

Because we have to save the giants.

The giants need me--us--to save them.

Ull's parents clearly know something about all of this, and I'm determined to find out what's afoot. So, I keep quiet, and I watch them. I don't budge from the small, wooden chair I'm perched on.

"Alright," Mr. Troll says, cracking his knuckles a bit before placing his hands, palm-down, flat on the table. "To explain what you're going to need to do, I'm going to have to explain what has already been done long before now."

I notice that Ull leans forward just a bit, lifting his dark silvery eyebrows.

Mr. Troll takes a breath and glances at Mrs. Troll. She nods encouragingly. He sighs. "I was there when it all happened, when the Mystic sent the giants out. We," he looked at his wife, "were sent to watch them and wait for the ones who would come to aid in the giants' return. "

The Mystic--I can hear the capital letter in his tone as he speaks it.

"The Mystic--is she the satyress?" Wink asks, eyes wide.

The Trolls look surprised. "You know of Mystic Tarek?" Mrs. Troll says in surprise.

Wink and I exchange glances. We explain about the book, the library, and how sometimes we just know things. We stumble over each others' words, trying to explain that we already know we're meant to find the staff. Ull gives a little gasp when we've finished, and he leans towards us resting his chin in his hands. "You're amazing," he tells us.

A *forest troll* who speaks *all languages* thinks that *we're* cool. Wink and I laugh. The trolls laugh, too, even though they don't know what's funny.

It's good to have so many people laughing. I am not used to hearing laughter like this. My house is always so quiet.

The giants never laugh.

When the laughter has died down, Ull's father stands up. "It was foretold that humans would help us reopen the way to our homeland, and that it would happen when the giants were ready." Mr. and Mrs. Troll exchange small smiles.

"They're ready," I whisper. "They're lonely, and they see what they did wrong."

No one nods, but everyone might as well have. The cold cavern air seems to hang gently around us, waiting for a moment before it begins to move again.

Mr. Troll sighs. "I suppose I should give you the map now." He glances at Mrs. Troll, then turns to Ull. "It's time to return," he says.

It's-beginning, it's-beginning, it's-beginning.

It's beginning, and I think that's a good thing. Maybe it's the best thing. I don't know; I can't be sure.

XII.

We are handed a map--it's a worn scroll, the type you read about or see in the movies. My breath catches in my throat. I'm terrified that I'm dreaming--but then I glance at Wink and know that she's real, and she's here--and she's afraid that she's dreaming too.

The scroll is in Ull's hands, then Wink's, only to find rest in mine. I cradle it in my arms, like it's a child--although, of course, I am the child. And it is old. It is so very, very old--crumbling at the edges. I feel like it is whispering hopes and fears to me--like I could whisper back and it would comfort me. It *is* comforting me, maybe.

I'm not sure.

I can't remember the last time I really felt comforted.

"Unroll it," Mrs. Troll says to me, gently placing her hand on my arm. I stiffen, but only a very little bit. I swallow, nod, and unroll it as gently as Mrs. Troll touched my arm, as gently as the giants blink, as gently as spring becomes summer.

It is beautiful like a painting--I turn to Wink, for she knows paintings. "Look," I say, holding it out to her. Splashes of colors, lines, and words in deep midnight-blue ink. It's like no map I have ever seen before. I can't even tell what it's a map *of.*

"Is this the mountain?" Wink asks skeptically, though her fingers are twitching like they do when she very deeply wants to touch a work of art. "It doesn't look like the mountain."

Mr. and Mrs. Troll exchange glances and Mrs. Troll pats my arm reassuringly. "The Mystic said it would make sense to those it needed to make sense to."

Wink and I look at each other and I feel sudden panic rising in my chest. It doesn't make sense to me. I have done something wrong.

Ull leans across the table and calmly takes the map from me as he mouths something to me that I can not make out. Though I don't know what he has said, I think it is something safe. I think he is making it safe somehow.

He strokes the map. He does not seem at all afraid to touch it as Wink and I are. He whispers to it, holding his lips close. He is breathing on it, he is breathing it in--he leans close enough to brush his lashes across it.

Wink and I watch, bewildered. His parents seem unsuprised and unamused. He must be like this all the time.

"Oh," he cries, as though he has fallen in love with someone he can never truly be near. "Oh, it's nearly time." He stands up and his voice rises in pitch as urgency seems to take over his tone. "You can both come into the woods tomorrow evening, yes? And be prepared to travel through the night, to wait 'til dawn to rest?"

Wink and I are unable to answer, blinking at him, our mouths hanging open.

"Ull," his father says, "explain?"

Ull puts a hand on his chest. "I can *guide* you," he whispers. "I know I can."

XIII.

Wink and I are headed home--Ull has taken us to the place where he found us, smiles, and waves good-bye. I wave back shyly.

I look at Wink. "Hey," I say, as though we haven't been together all day. "Want one of the cookies?"

Ull's mom has sent us home with cookies and sandwiches. We've eaten the sandwiches, but saved the cookies. I'm carrying them in a small linen drawstring bag.

"I suppose," she says quietly.

I hand her one, and watch her eating it for a few moments before I ask. "Are you okay?"

She closes her eyes. "Yeah."

I feel like she's lying to me, but I hate to think that. After all, she is my best friend, and we've promised to be there for each other always. I feel guilty. I hand her another cookie for atonement, though she has no idea what's going through my head.

She pushes it back to me, looking concerned. "Are *you* okay?"

"I always am," I promise, but it feels a little hollow. She squints at me. "Well, sometimes," I amend.

She casts her eyes to the ground. "I'm going to tell my mom we're going on a camping adventure."

I take a bite out of my cookie. It tastes like cinnamon and caramel and honey. It's difficult to smile and eat at the same time, but I do. I swallow. "We've never gone on a camping adventure," I say.

She nods. "And this will be the biggest camping adventure."

"Will she think it's weird if you don't bring a sleeping bag?" I ask.

Wink shrugs. "She might not even notice."

How? I want to ask. *And what if she does?*

I don't.

I take another bite out of the cookie.

I shove one hand in my pocket.

I clench my fist.

"Peri?" Wink says, a second later. "You got quiet, are you sure you're okay?"

I unclench my fist. "Yes," I say. "I just feel quieter these days, I guess." *The giants are quiet. My house is quiet.*

And now I am quiet as well.

I freeze up, but then Wink is grabbing my hand. "Hey," she says, seriously, "please don't go all quiet and sad, Peri, not like the giants."

Maybe she *does* know what I am thinking. Because, sometimes, we both just know things.

We reach her house sooner than I'd like. I stare at the road. I can feel the presence of the giants suddenly, and I am fearful. I had forgotten them for a while. I can hear one breathing just beyond my sight.

"Can you walk home by yourself?" Wink asks softly. It is getting dark.

What if I say no? Will she come with me? Will I stay here?

But I want to seem *very* strong and brave.

And, after all, I'm used to being alone.

Knowing I'll hate myself for this later, I nod. "Of course I can," I say. It's surprising to me how normal this sounds coming out of my mouth when everything inside of me feels deathly still.

Wink looks hurt and steps back. "If you want to stay, you can," she says. "We can make a fort in my room. My sisters won't mind."

I do want to, so much. More than anything. This is what I've been wanting for ages--to pretend to be one of the McCalls and just blend in with Wink and her siblings.

But I don't want to recant. I feel committed.

"It's okay," I promise. I want to seem like the brave one.

She looks at the ground. "Okay," she says. She turns around and runs into her house.

I stand there, gravel crunching beneath my feet. I regret not being honest with her.

I feel regret more than I've ever felt anything in my life.

I could probably go to the door and knock, and she'd answer it and let me in. And I would be safe.

I can hear the giants' breathing. I can feel the darkness settling in around me. I am hungry. My heart starts hammering in my chest.

I run home as quickly as I can, always wishing that someone would stop me since I can't seem to stop myself.

Near my driveway, I stumble and fall. Can't stop myself. Gravel flies and I can already feel my hands smarting from fresh scrapes. I blink dust out of my eyes, trying not to cry.

I fail.

I should've gone home with Wink.

I curl up on the ground and cry. I know a giant is sitting there watching me. I know it, and I hate it, and I hate everything.

I hate the giants for not being able to actually be near me. I hate my parents for never being there. I hate Wink for being all of the things I am not. I hate myself for existing.

I cry and I cry and I cry, but the driveway stays as dry and dusty and lifeless as ever.

My dad always said tears didn't accomplish anything.

I'm not sure about that, but they definitely haven't accomplished much right now.

I sit up, feeling a different kind of frenzy than earlier. *I'm sorry.* I turn to the giant. "I don't really hate you," I tell him. "I'm so, so sorry. I'll still help you, I promise, if you want it."

He just watches me sadly like always. But then he nods. He gets up. He lumbers away, disappearing in the trees.

I should apologize to Wink. I should call my parents--they left the number for the hotel they'd be basing out of--and leave an apology message. It occurs to me that I could apologize to myself, but I think that sounds ridiculous. Why *that* is ridiculous and calling a hotel miles away isn't? I don't know.

My heart rate had slowed when I was crying, but it's picked back up again and I feel shaky. I drag myself into the house and collapse on the loveseat.

Somehow, I manage to start to drift off to sleep, even though it feels like everything inside of me is stifling screams. It's a bit relieving, though I can't stop a little voice in my head from telling me that I should feel bad about this. That I deserve no relief, ever. I try to shut the voice up as best I can, and I suppose I succeed because I feel myself falling more and more into the sweet blackness of sleep.

XIV.

I wake up still feeling exhausted which does not bode well for a long hiking trip.

I realize with a sinking feeling in my stomach that I'm alone until evening.

I probably could go to Wink's, I think to myself, lying there and staring at the ceiling boards. They are white, though slightly discolored due to years of remaining the same while home decor trends change.

I could probably go to Wink's.

Wink probably wouldn't mind, I reason with myself. *She might be excited! I could walk there quickly--I might make breakfast!* I jump up, suddenly feeling excited and refreshed. I can almost hear Mrs. McCall saying it's a pleasant surprise for me to turn up. I can almost see Wink's surprised and happy face. Maybe she could teach me how to paint mini tree frogs like she does.

But the dream crashes quickly. She also might be upset with me for not coming over last night. She might not even want to go on the adventure--or quest--hiking trip--with me and Ull tonight.

I honestly can't picture Wink being upset about this. But she *could be,* and it's the *could-be* that holds me back. It's the could-be that keeps me at home all day, wandering listlessly, and staring the giants down. I look at them through the window, a different giant every few hours, and I wish they could talk to me. I wish anyone were there to talk. Wink could be there, but of course--No.

I stop that train of thought very quickly. I stifle it, like I'm shoving it into a box and smothering it, smothering it, smothering it.

It doesn't *matter* why I'm here alone. It doesn't matter if it's my choice or not, I just *am.* That should be enough. I should stop thinking about it. I should stop thinking. I should stop. I should.

That's how I spend the morning, in a constant state of upheaval, trying to keep my mind as quiet as possible. Ignoring the quiet, watching eyes of the giants. Crying into the couch cushions.

It's not really all that different from normal, honestly, just a little more uncomfortable.

And maybe that's what happened. I let myself get too comfortable. I had felt at home, out there in the forest, headed up the mountain.

Then there's a knock at the door.

I barely get the door open before Wink is hugging me very, very tightly. "The phone wasn't working," she gasped, "I ran all the way here because I wanted to make sure you survived last night."

I feel very warm and very cold all at once. I can't believe I thought she was mad at me.

"Of course I survived," I say, "because I'm a super-tough explorer. I wrestled seven bears on the way home last night, as per usual."

Wink laughs.

I laugh, too, and it's mostly relief. I don't have to keep distracting myself now--Wink is here! And she isn't mad, not at all-- or, if she is, she's hiding it.

"You're the best wrestler ever," she says. "I know you've been training very hard to be a champion wrestler."

This is the farthest thing from the truth. I am small--I have been called *shrimpy* before. She lightly punches my arm and I laugh harder.

"My mom couldn't believe I let you walk home alone. Of course, we knew you'd be fine, but we also worried. It's confusing."

I know what she means, and I'm very tempted to tell her that nothing was fine until she knocked on the door. That's why I just hug her again, very, very tightly.

"Come on," she says. "We're having brunch."

I've never had brunch, but I decide right then and there that it is the best possible thing in the world.

"We have to eat a lot of brunch to be ready for," she wiggles her eyebrows, "our totally-not-suspicious camping trip."

"It has *nothing* to do with quests," I add, "nothing *at all.*"

"Right," she says. "That would be ridiculous. Unbelievable, really." Then she squints at me. "Are you… aren't those the same clothes you wore yesterday?"

I pull away, stumbling back very quickly. I laugh nervously. "Um, yeah, I just hadn't gotten around to changing, yet."

"Okay," she says, calmly. "You go change and, if we run, we can still make it back for brunch!"

She's being the brave, in-charge one again. Part of me feels like I'm losing a battle; I'm also too tired to keep fighting.

I just go change.

Everything changes.

XV.

Brunch is good, but I do feel like I should've enjoyed it more than I did. I feel like I should've carried conversation better, too. Been more awake. Been more excitable. But, being excitable is tiring, and I was already very tired. Existing will do that to you, sometimes.

Now I'm sitting in the bedroom that Wink shares with her two older sisters, and I'm watching Wink paint. She's painting on a *canvas.* I didn't know she did that. I'd seen her pinkie nail art, but never this. I'm not sure how to feel about not having known. She's *good.* Very good. She's painting the interior of the Trolls' house--the room with the table, the room where we were handed the map.

Ull has the map now. It only made sense for him to have it, since he was the only one that it seemed to make any sense to. I yawn and Wink glances my way. "You need a nap?" she asks. "Remember, Ull wanted us to be up all night, for whatever reason. You should be well-rested, you know? You can borrow my bed or the couch."

I sit on my hands. "Um," I say, slowly, "thank you, but I think I'll be fine."

She shrugs and goes back to painting.

I do drift off a bit, sitting there, but manage to feign alertness whenever she speaks. Her siblings filter in and out of the room, occasionally mussing my hair or poking my arms. They smile at me encouragingly. They talk loudly.

It's everything I imagined, but I find myself uncomfortable with the sound of it all. I miss the quiet. I miss it, so much.

When afternoon comes, Wink and I gather up a few supplies--food, water bottles, flashlights--and head outside, waving goodbye to her family.

"Be back by dinnertime tomorrow, girls," Mrs. McCall reminds us.

We nod, though we aren't sure we'll be able to keep this promise.

As we walk away, Wink speaks in a low, conspiratorial tone. "Now you see," she mumbles. "Can't get any peace."

I *do* see, but I also think that perhaps, if I had another chance to be surrounded by cacophony of existing familial love, I might enjoy it. Just maybe. I'd have to try it again. When I wasn't… whatever it is I am today. Myself.

Wink elbows me. "Peri," she says, "don't be so quiet, we're outside! Not in a library!"

I laugh. Well, I try to.

"Peri," she says again, dragging my name out very long and very low. "Fearless adventurer Peri, are you ready to enter the woods? We are preparing to go on the most amazing of quests, in order to save the giants from… from… from the punishment they earned long ago." She shrugs her small shoulders beneath her backpack straps. Then she does an announcer voice. "Peri, brave enough to walk home alone!"

I laugh, and now it's my turn to elbow her. I'm not sure it was brave that made me walk home alone, but I'll roll with it.

We march into the forest, and I do feel a tiny bit better.

We hear a tree frog calling. I recognize the sound from when Wink first told me about them not too long ago. We exchange small smiles and chirp back to the tree frog before giggling.

"I like tree frogs," she says.

"I know you do," I smile. "I remember."

The tree frog has gone silent, but we decide that maybe it just got distracted. We speculate--maybe it was having lunch, maybe it was taking a dance break, maybe it was enamored with another frog's appearance and had forgotten how to speak. There's a lot of giggling and smiling and shoving each other playfully as we continue to the place Ull told us to meet him. When we get to the spot, we both instinctively go quiet.

Ull isn't there yet, so we sit down. I'm feeling less tired now. Having a good time will do that to you, sometimes, you know?

"This is exciting," Wink tells me. I agree. "I'm glad you're here," she says.

"I'm glad you're here, too," I say.

A quiet rustling in the bushes. We whip around--but it's only Ull. He laughs like we are the funniest creatures he has ever seen and nods at us happily. "We're ready," he says, but it feels like he's promising.

I like that promise. I already feel much safer. Much, much safer than I did at home by myself with the giants watching me.

Speaking of the giants--I pause to listen for them. One is definitely nearby. I hear him sighing.

I will help you--we all will, I promise him in my mind. I hope the thought reaches him and feels as promise-safe as Ull's statement did.

Poor, lonely giants.

It's beginning, or, no--it's begun. We can do it, we can do it, if I can only....

XVI.

We are going. It's an adventure, or a quest, but maybe a journey, or... All of them at once. Does it need a name? It's a dream, a hope fulfilled, and a prayer; and that's what's so beautiful and brave about it.

We've been telling Ull about our human lives-- I think mine sounds boring compared to Wink's, but he seems equally interested.

"I've always wanted a sibling," he says. "Or maybe I haven't. I honestly don't know." He smiles at us, then squints down at the map. Conversation over, for now.

He says confusing things a lot, but acts like they're perfectly normal things to say. Like they make sense. I admire that quality, just a bit. It's cool and a bit comforting--calming, even. I'm not sure why.

He keeps stroking the map, pressing his face against it, rubbing it up and down his arms. This seems to be how he's reading it, somehow. Occasionally he'll hum or sing a few notes in a language I don't understand. Then he'll point in the distance, "Let's go that way!"

Wink and I follow him. Neither of us is leader now. And that's okay.

The forest is beautiful, and it only seems to get more beautiful the deeper we go. It gets chillier as it gets later in the day and as we go further up the mountain. We walk for what feels like forever, only stopping for snacks sometimes.

When Wink and I run out of water, we become nervous.

"Peri," Wink says, but then she goes deathly quiet. She bites her lip and looks at me out of the corner of her eye.

I'm not sure what that's about, but I know what she had been going to ask Ull. Sometimes we both just know things. So I ask him.

"Ull, where can we get water?" I say, softly.

Ull turns around, seeming very surprised. He closes his eyes and points to the right. "That way."

Wink and I exchange glances. Should we go alone or get him to lead?

He opens his eyes and they seem much brighter suddenly. Frantic energy is behind them. "Follow me," he demands.

He dashes through the forest suddenly.

"He's like a soda you shook and then opened," Wink says.

I nod, laughing.

We follow him, running, skipping, lighter than light, lighter than air.

When we find him, he's crouched at a very small stream, washing his face. The map sticks slightly out of his backpack.

"You're sure this water is safe?" Wink asks.

Ull stands up a bit straighter. "That water is safer than the water you drink in the comfort of your home, I'm sure."

We nod, then set to filling our water bottles. When we've finished, I stand again and see Ull wrinkling his nose at the bottles. "What's wrong?" I ask.

"Well," he says. "I just--can't you taste the plastic when you drink from those?"

Wink and I exchange glances, then shake our heads. Of course we can't.

He shrugs, then pulls the map out. He squints at it. "We can take a shortcut from here, if you'd like."

I've read lots of adventure books, plus my parents are always off on adventures. I've heard things. I know things. "Shortcuts always make it take longer," I tell him. "Wink has to be home. We can't do that." I glance at Wink, hoping she'll see that I'm taking care of her, being there for her.

Instead, she says rapidly, "I don't have to be home. We can do whatever."

Do I flinch? Do I tear up? Does this make me uncomfortable?

Yes.

Does anyone notice?

No. I'm good at hiding things, sometimes. How often have I had to hide a shiver caused by a giant's stare, hide my tears when my parents leave, hide my frustration when Wink doesn't call?

I am very used to this.

"I don't mind either way," Ull says, still gazing at the map adoringly. "This is a wonderful map," he says.

I still think it looks like an explosion of nonsense, but I'm glad he likes it so very much.

He glances up. "Let's take the shortcut," he says.

I have a bad feeling about this.

I roll with it anyway.

XVII.

It's getting late, when Ull says we should stop to eat. He says this, giving the map a long lick before he rolls it up. We wrinkle our noses. Wink and I are unsure--we'd like to save our food, even though we are quite hungry now. Before we can say anything, though, he has taken his bag off of his back and is loosening the drawstrings to pull packages out. "Are cucumber sandwiches something humans eat? And do humans happen to like smoked venison?" he asks with deep concern. "Mother was afraid you wouldn't." Wink and I assure him that humans certainly do eat cucumber sandwiches and smoked venison. He smiles. "My family will be delighted to hear that," he declares. Then he pulls out another package. "And, of course, we knew you liked cookies--that's a fact." He unwraps the package to reveal more cookies, similar to what we had yesterday.

Wink applauds this revelation, and Ull flinches, leaning away from her. "What's wrong?" Wink asks, quickly.

He looks confused. "Clapping," he says, quietly. "It means to stop, doesn't it?"

"No," I say. "Not for us, at least. It more means, *do it again.*"

"Sometimes it can mean to stop," Wink says, thoughtfully. "But not usually, and not this time."

"Oh," Ull says. He looks at the ground. "I didn't know," he said. "It's different for trolls, I guess." He looks at the ground.

"What would we have been telling you to stop?" I ask, stepping a bit closer to him.

"I rhyme," he sighs. "Or, sometimes it's a slant rhyme. When I'm feverish, I speak in alliteration." This seems to have taken a lot out of him, and he sits down on the ground.

Wink and I sit down, too.

"I hadn't even noticed," I tell him--and it's true. Looking back, now, I realize he has been speaking in rhymes, sometimes. Then I realize that I have just thought a rhyme. I would share it, if I weren't comforting him.

"And I like it," Wink says.

"It's a bad habit," Ull says rapidly. "No one will ever take me seriously as a BridgeKeeper if I rhyme all the time."

He used the same rhyme! This strikes me as hilarious, but I don't share it. I bite my lip.

"Well," Wink says, and she looks at me out of the corner of her eye. "You do lick maps."

Ull looks confused. "What do you mean, I lick maps? Just this map. No shame in that, it was meant to be licked."

"Well," she says, "I just don't think it would be easy to take you seriously ever, knowing you'd done that."

He looks deeply wounded.

"I take it seriously that you licked it," I say thoughtfully. "You know, because it was... It meant something. It needed to be done, somehow."

"People will either take you seriously or they won't," Wink says. "It doesn't change who you are." A funny look comes into her eye. "And who are we all?"

"We're saving the giants," I whisper.

"We're going on a quest," Wink says.

"We're hungry," Ull announces.

And, thus, the conversation is over. It's almost like it never even happened.

We eat sandwiches--and the cucumbers taste fresher than anything I've eaten in ages. When my parents are gone, I mostly have canned food--they stockpile it for me, so that I have something to eat while they're gone. I usually don't even think about it, but after eating with Wink's family and the Trolls... and now this...

I never want to go home.

I'm also terrified that I should go home, right now, before I get more used to this. Before I like it more. Before I get too attached.

It's wonderful, though, to be laughing and smiling and eating sandwiches and discussing magic and invisible giants without anyone looking at you like you've completely lost your mind. Ull confides that he saw his first giant when he was seven. "I don't see them, so much, anymore," he says. "And, when I do, they don't scare me as much. I understand them better."

I open my mouth to say that I understand them, too--but, do I? I'm not sure.

I thought I did, but if I did, maybe I would be less scared of them, less frustrated with them. Maybe this would all be less difficult. Maybe I wouldn't be so tired.

I consider this as I eat my cookie.

"Alright," Ull says, when we're all finished and the conversation has died. "Now." He pulls the map out once more and brushes his lashes across it. "Yes," he says. "I think we're nearly there."

"Nearly to the place the staff is?" I ask.

"Oh, no," he says. "Goodness, no. But we are nearly to the first trial."

"Trial?" Wink and I gasp, shocked. No one said anything about trials.

He nods, shivering with excitement. "The Hall of Ghosts," he murmurs. "I've only heard about it in stories." He begins packing up the food.

"What's the Hall of Ghosts?" I dare whisper.

He looks up at me and Wink with his silvery eyes shining in the dusk-nearing-dark. "It's actually a cave. You'll see. You'll see very soon."

I don't like the sound of that, not at all. Something in the way he says it makes me feel as though a dark, wet sheet has settled on my shoulders. It's a scary feeling.

We have been walking for a long time, our flashlights shining in the dark, when Ull suddenly stops. Wink and I almost run into him.

"Okay," he says, whispering. "Are either of you afraid of caves?"

I've never been in a cave before. Wink has, but she was only seven. I don't know if either of us is prepared to not be afraid. I swallow. "Um, I don't know," I try to whisper, but my throat is dry and nothing comes out.

"Keep your flashlights on," he tells us. "I'm a troll, we're used to caves."

"I thought you'd never been here before," Wink says shakily. The cool night air whistling around the mountain makes everything much scarier. "I don't understand."

"I've been in caves before, just not this one." He starts to head into what Wink and I now can see to be an opening in the side of the mountain--just big enough for a person our size to squeeze through.

"Wait," I call, before he disappears into it. He pauses, one foot in the dark mouth of the cave. "Why is it called the Hall of Ghosts? What makes it a trial?"

Ull takes a deep breath.

"It's called the Hall of Ghosts because of an old story. It takes place back when beings could slip between your world and the magic world with no worry. This cave was for the bravest of the mages who would see if their bravery could withstand the ages. Each story is different, each experience unique--so I can't tell you what it's like until our adventure is complete." He swallows. "It's going to be hard, though. All the stories say that time seems to warp in this cave. It's like you're floating in time, confused and lost and alone. I don't know, though. I've only heard the stories my dad tells."

I can hear Wink swallowing hard. "So, we won't know we're with each other?"

"Maybe not," he says. "But as long as you keep walking, you'll make it out. We all will."

"Then how is it a trial?" I ask.

Ull looks sheepish in the light of my flashlight. "Well, it kind of determines if you're willing to go on the rest of the quest or not."

Oh, I think, but don't say. I watch as he slowly steps into the cave mouth. He seems almost excited to be running into danger and fright. Wink grabs my hand. "We can do this," she promises. "We're brave adventurers!"

I don't feel very brave right now, but I nod anyway. "The bravest," I agree in a whisper.

We step in after Ull.

The floor of the cave is a little bit slick with stalactites and stalagmites--visible only by the beam of our flashlights--reaching for each other in the dark, looking like petrified icicles. They *are* petrified icicles in a way, I suppose.

I squeeze Wink's hand. She squeezes back because we're in this together.

Ull is spinning. His bare troll feet must not feel the cold or the wet and must maintain better traction than our shoed human feet do. "Turn off your flashlights," he demands. "Turn them off."

This goes against everything I know to do--definitely against my better judgement. Surely Wink feels the same way.

And yet--

And yet, we turn off our flashlights. Click, click.

We are bathed in suffocating blackness. My heart starts beating faster. I squeeze Wink's hand again, tighter.

"I'm still here," she promises, a slight tremor in her voice.

"Ull?" I call. My voice echoes a bit, and I can hear slight dripping. "Ull?"

A demented-sounding giggle in the distance. Then a sob.

"Ull?" I whisper. I try to stand very still. I don't know what's in the cave, I don't know where I'm going. Was that Ull, or someone... something... else?

Wink nudges me, and I almost lose my balance. Funny how not being able to see can do that to you. "We have to keep walking," she whispers. "Remember what Ull said?"

Ull, surely, was wrong. I shake my head, though it's too dark for her to see. "No," I whisper furiously. "No, I'm staying here until daylight."

Wink pulls her hand from mine, and I feel even more unsteady than I did before. "What about the *giants,* Peri?" she demands. "They need us to do this." When I don't say anything, she gets louder. "What about the *Trolls?* They need to get home, too!" I know she's right, but I don't feel like she *can* be right. So I remain silent. "Fine," she says after a moment. "You're always so scared."

The words are a slap, but so is the fact that her voice is getting farther away. "Wink!" I cry finally when it's too late. Or--is it? How long has it been since she spoke?

Are those her footsteps I can hear?

I take cautious steps finding that my entire perspective feels warped, my entire body off-balance. Are those Wink's footsteps still?

Can I catch up to her if I move perfectly quickly and carefully?

I try, but I keep losing my balance. Suddenly I can't tell if I'm leaning against the cave wall or the floor. This isn't normal in-the-dark disorientation. This must be the trial that Ull was talking about.

I crawl or walk leaning against the wall, or--something. I move. I move forward, and that's what matters.

I'm trying to catch up with Wink. I have to catch up with Wink because she's leaving me behind. I can't let Wink leave me behind--

"Peri?"

I freeze. That's my *mom's* voice. My heart hammers in my chest as I swear that the earth tilts beneath me. "Mama?" I call. Then I curse myself because, of course, she's not here. I'm in a cave. This is part of the trial.

"Peri," I hear again. "Peri, love." It's *definitely* her voice. I run through ways it would be possible for her to be here, each idea more impossible and outlandish than the last. Deep down, I know it's just the cave magic. But I so badly wish it weren't.

That's when I remember the name of the cave and it feels like something breaks inside of me.

The Hall of Ghosts.

Mama isn't a ghost.

My heart hammers in my chest.

She's *alive.* They've just been off exploring. And they haven't called because they never do because they don't worry about me. Because I can take care of myself. Because, I'm---

"So very grown-up." That's Dad's voice. That's what he said when they left.

That's what he has always, always said when they started to leave. This time, since it was the first time I was left completely alone, he said it twice.

"So grown up. So very grown-up, Peri-love."

I wish I didn't have to be grown-up, ever. I wish I hadn't been being grown-up, and I wish I didn't have to be grown-up now.

"Mama," I cry, "Daddy."

Of course, no one comes.

No one could come.

There's no one there.

I HAVE to do this on my own. I have to make it out. The giants are counting on me. The trolls are counting on me. Wink and Ull are ahead waiting for me.

So, inch by inch, I work my way forward--though I can't tell up and down, left and right, I can tell forward and backwards. I think maybe that's part of the cave magic--like, maybe the cave is rooting for me, but telling me that moving forward is all that matters right now. That I CAN make it out. Pressing myself against the stone surface, I feel rough rock scrape my cheek as I move. I wonder if I'm bleeding.

Not that it matters, really--who is going to see me or worry about me?

"Peri," another voice calls. This time Wink's. Is it the real Wink or a ghost Wink? I don't dare call out again--another false hope will make me cry, I'm certain of it.

"Peri, don't you love the quiet?" Wink's voice continues. "Don't you like it? Aren't you glad to be alone?"

I stifle a sob and keep pushing forwards. I am brave, though I shouldn't have to be. And I do not love the quiet. The giants have to experience so, so much quiet, and they shouldn't have to be brave and alone in it. So, as I move forward, I am fighting the silence. I am fighting the loneliness. I am fighting the fear.

I am pushing, I am fighting, and I am also running. I'm running from something, I'm not sure what. Maybe I'm also running from… from being scared.

Wink says I've always been scared.

And I don't want to be scared anymore.

XVIII.

Somehow I make it out of the cave alive, though I am not sure how. I am panting and my face is tear streaked--and, from feeling it, probably dirty and bleeding, too. I lie in the cave exit for a moment feeling pale moonlight on my face. I'm in a clearing,now--there's no telling how far I've come, how much ground I've covered.

Finally, I sit up, wiping my eyes. I turn on my flashlight. "Wink? Ull?" I call.

I hear excited gasps. Part of me is hurt down deep inside that they made it through before I did. Like, maybe it wasn't as hard for them. But I am roo relieved and proud of myself to REALLY care. They come running to the entrance. "Peri," Wink gasps, her eyes bright with an odd sort of energy I've never seen before. Then she hugs me very, very tightly. She looks mostly fine, like maybe she has gotten a bit damp and scared and grimy, but isn't altogether unwell. Like she will recover in a moment's time.

Ull, however, looks much worse off. His silver skin is nearly white and not very sparkly at all. He has dark circles. He is shaking. I stare at him with wide, concerned eyes, but he quickly offers me a smile.

I sigh the longest sigh ever, possibly.

"We made it," Ull says, shakily. It is strange to me that he should look so frightened and hurt and tired when he was so excited to experience this before. "It was hard, I admit."

But he's rhyming. So he must be okay. He is still himself.

Wink releases me from her embrace slowly. We look into each other's eyes--I search her dark chocolate eyes for some explanation of what happened to her.

Her eyes only reveal that she is much, much more upset that she seems... and that she will not be sharing why with me, at least, not right now.

That's okay.

I'm not sharing right now, either.

Ull, however, is very much in the mood to share his troubles. And, as we start walking again--he says we should continue--he explains.

"I don't think I *want* to be a BridgeKeeper," he announces. Then he glances around as though terrified that someone might've heard him.

Wink and I are silent, following him through the woods, our feet slipping and crunching on pine needles and leaves.

"What other job could a troll have?" Wink asks finally.

Ull shakes his head quickly and roughly. "I don't know," he says. "I don't know what I could do or where I could go."

Don't-go-don't-go, a small voice in my head whispers. I blink hard to get it to go away.

He isn't humming or swaying now. He's walking quickly and it's a bit difficult for me to keep up. Wink is having similar trouble. We are tired. I am incredibly tired from earlier and also from the trial. A horrible thought strikes me. "There isn't another trial, is there, Ull?" I ask, my voice squeaking a bit.

He glances over his shoulder at me, his eyes sorry. "There's one more," he says. "But it shouldn't take long."

My breath catches in my throat and I feel like throwing up. Can I handle another trial? I suppose I have to, but how can I? I try to feel the resolve I found in the cave--and it's still there, though less strong. The giants still need me. The Trolls still need me.

"You know what I'd like to do," Ull says softly in a hollow-sounding voice-- several minutes later, when I think we have moved on-- "I'd like to sing."

Wink stops walking. "Sing?"

Ull turns around and his little spark of madness is back dancing in his eyes. He smiles a tired smile. "I could sing our story," he tells us. He looks in her eyes, then mine. "And the giants' story. And it might help someone someday." He stands up a bit straighter. "That's what I want."

I ask the obvious question, falteringly. "Then… then who would keep the bridges."

Ull glances at the ground. "I'm sure someone else could do it," he murmurs. "Just because no other troll family ever has kept the bridges doesn't mean that they can't."

"You could write song bridges," I muse. But I don't realize I've said it out loud until I realize Ull and Wink are giggling and applauding.

Ull nods, saying that's exactly what he'll do (it's true, must be true). When we start walking again, Wink says, "Peri's good like that," like I'm not there.

I wonder what *good like that* is. Though I don't know, I like it. I feel a little bit proud, and I smile at the backs of their heads.

I'm good like that.

XIX.

It's kind of an unspoken rule that we won't be asking about the next trial. Ull licks and caresses his map, leading us on a twisting path further up the mountain. Our flashlights are getting dim.

I do ask one question.

"Are we going to the top?" This seems to me like the perfect place for us to be headed to. That's exactly where the staff would be hidden in a fairy story. Of course, this isn't a fairy story. It's a giants and trolls and satyresses and Peri and Wink story.

"Oh, no," Ull says. "After all, this isn't a fairy story."

Wink gasps. At the same time, she and I chorus, "That's what I was thinking!"

Ull laughs a high, clear laugh. "Wonderful," he says. "It isn't a fairy story, it's our story. Our tale. Which is why, my friends," and he says this with a brave, loud air, "we must prevail!"

We are not whispering in the woods; this is partially to keep ourselves from imagining things in the silence and partially to keep away things in the silence. It feels a bit sacrilegious, though. I'm nearly afraid the forest will cave in around me as punishment for breaking the sanctity of the stillness of the night.

When it's near dawn, we hear water trickling in the distance, and it occurs to me that we have reached the next trial. I don't know how I know. Sometimes I just know things.

"Ull," Wink says quietly. "We're there, aren't we?"

We are looking at a big, clear pool. In the distance, we can hear little mountain streams trickling down, down, down on paths they've been on for years.

I can't see the bottom of the pool because it's a perfect mirror of the sky and the spindly mountain pines. These pines aren't pink--there are fewer pink pines the further up we go. These pines are deep, deep green--and there are other trees, now, like spruces and cedars. The pool is too pretty to be called a pond, but too small to be a lake. The surface is smooth, crystal clear.

Ull takes a deep breath. "Yes," he says, "we're here. And we're going to have to swim to the bottom."

My eyes go wide. "How deep is it?" I'm not a strong swimmer. I only learned to swim two summers ago when my parents were home. I can go to the bottom of the swimming pool in town--but I'm not sure I can go farther.

Ull shrugs. "It's magical," he says, as though that should comfort me.

Wink shrugs. "No problem," she says. "I've been swimming since I was four. I'm going to be a lifeguard when I'm older. I can handle this."

Ull shrugs again. "It's magical," he says, as though that should frighten her.

I stare at the pool. "Why do we have to swim to the bottom?" I ask.

"Some call it the Glass of Realization," he says. "Though, to me, that sounds like idealization. You make it to the bottom, and then you see... things that may or may not be." He looks surprised. "Oh, Father says there are supposed to be keys down there. Keys placed by the Mystic fair."

We exchanged excited looks, all three of us. We know what that must mean. These keys must help us to get to the staff, which is what we need to open the portal back to the world of the giants and trolls and pink-and-purple pines.

Ull slips his bag off of his back and rolls the map up, placing it safely inside. Wink and I click off our flashlights--the sun is coming up, anyways--and place our backpacks on the ground next to his. We slip off our socks and shoes.

Ull smiles at us and dives in easily. Wink grins, takes a deep breath, and does the same.

I stare at the pool for a minute and then close my eyes. Deep breaths.

I can do this.

I don't dive in like Ull and Wink had. I step in and shudder at the cold. The cold is like the quiet in a way. It's not an unfamiliar feeling.

I slip into the water, letting myself sink for a few moments before I start swimming down. Sure enough, now that I'm in the water, I can see the bottom of the pool--and something shiny.

So focused am I on swimming towards the shiny thing, it's a few seconds before I think to look for Wink and Ull. I glance around, but don't see them. This frightens me so much that I start swimming back up, back to the surface.

But then I feel as though something is pulling me down frighteningly quickly. I don't have much air. My heart hammers in my chest, and I keep trying to pull myself up desperately.

Come on, Peri, I think to myself. Oddly enough, though, the exasperated voice in my head doesn't sound like me. It sounds like Wink. Maybe the magic makes us able to communicate, I wonder, and I think back, desperately, *I'm trying, Wink*

No response.

Wink?

Nothing.

I am dragged down further though my lungs are burning.

Maybe the magic is drowning me. Maybe I deserve it, somehow. Maybe I'm dying and I should be dying. Maybe Wink and Ull are meant to save the giants and not me. Where are they? Why aren't they coming to help? Why is no one ever coming to help?

Then I remember that Wink invited me to her house when I was scared, and I said no. And I think, *this is why I'm drowning.* The voice in my head sounds more like me again. But so, so tired. And I *am* tired. And maybe I should tell someone that and then they'll come help.

And then my feet hit the squishy, sandy bottom--my toes tangling in some sort of aquatic plants, sinking into the earth. That's when I realize--I am breathing. I'm underwater, but I'm breathing normally, and I can see clearly, and my lungs aren't burning anymore.

I glance down--and, sure enough, there it is. A shining, golden skeleton key, small and wonderfully wrought; it's waiting for me. It's been here for so long, waiting for me to finally come around and find it.

I pick up the key.

I am so tired; I should tell someone that.

It echoes in my head.

The next thing I know, I am breaking through the surface, gasping for air. It's bright, early morning. Birds are singing.

Wink and Ull are on the shore. They're applauding me.

Once again, I am the last to finish.

I bite my lip and pack away my frustration. It doesn't matter.

We have the keys.

We can save the giants.

We can help the trolls.

I forget to remember how tired I really, actually am.

At least… I tell myself I do.

XX.

"You did it, Peri!" Wink gasps. And she looks... terrible. Her hair is horrifically tangled, her eyes are frightened, her face is pale. And yet, she looks better than I feel, as always. Part of me admires her for that. I entertain, momentarily, a fantasy of demanding that she teach me how she always manages to look confident and capable despite all circumstances. Then I blink hard and pull myself out of the water. I shiver in the cool morning mountain air. Ull beams brightly-- he's looking more like himself than he had before the swim.

I wish I knew what had happened to them both times.

But I don't want to share what happened to me. I'm also afraid that mine was much worse or much easier than theirs and that somehow I'm doing this wrong.

So I don't even ask.

We all hold our keys up to the light-- they are identical, flashing in the morning sun.

We are *so* close.

Ull's hands and dark silvery curls are finally dry enough that he feels safe unrolling his beloved map. He presses his lips against it.

"Are you making out?" Wink whispers. I giggle. Ull snaps to attention.

"I'm *reading* it," he sighs. "It's a feelings map. It reads emotionally."

This is preposterous, of course, even in a world with pink-and-purple pine trees, trolls, and giants. So, of course, we laugh.

I've never seen anyone look as hurt as Ull does in that moment. But then he straightens even more and thrusts the map out to us. "You try," he says forcefully.

We go quiet.

We can't, of course.

But we take it anyway, one side in my free hand and the other in Wink's. We hold it close to our faces trying to read it the way a map *should* be read. Of course, it's as impossible as the first time we tried it.

I'm the one who kisses it first. I press my lips against the crackly paper, right against a green smudge. Nothing happens.

Or does it? Because I'm confident that we're almost there, that it's time to run, that we have come so far.

And we should go…. *That way.* I giggle and look up at Ull. Relief washes over his face. "I told you," he murmurs. "And, after all, I have brought you this far."

Wink looks from me, to Ull, to the map. Suddenly she kisses it, too. I see confusion pass over her features, then assurance. She points north. "That way."

Doesn't north just feel right?

We have only dripped a few droplets of water on the map, but Ull winces and blows on them anyway. "It's okay," Ull says.

"They'll dry. The map has been on the adventure with us." He smiles and rolls it up. "We don't need it now. I know where we're going."

"North?" I ask, confused about how we will know how far north to go. He laughs.

"North Cave," he says. "If you'd read the map longer, you'd know. It's okay." He holds his key to the light again, and Wink and I mimic him. "We're nearly there," he says, in a soft, breathy tone. "It's really happening."

It *is* really happening, and that's all I can think of as we start back walking again once Wink and I have put our shoes on. Wet feet in dry shoes is an odd, but not completely unenjoyable feeling. I wiggle my toes. My shoes are very nice--my parents got them for me before they left on their last adventure. I realize, now, that perhaps they were trying to make up for leaving me again. At the time, I'd just been thrilled that they'd thought of me. There'd been a lot of that, now that I thought about it-- but I don't mind, actually. If they wanted to make it up to me, that means they did care. Right?

I glance at Wink. I wonder if she ever wonders if her parents love her, or if she always just knows. I've never asked. In fact, I never ask her much of anything… or tell her much of anything, either. Guilt creeps in because that's not how a friend should be. I push it back from the corners of my mind, looking at the key in my hand again. It's wonderful, really-- very pretty. I wish I could take a picture, to keep it forever. Then I realize that Wink could probably paint me a picture of it, and I decide that I would *greatly* prefer that. I jog a few steps to walk next to her.

"Wink," I say, excitedly, "could you do me a favor when we get home, I mean?" She glances my way looking pleasantly surprised. She nods. I take a deep breath. "Could you paint the keys?" I hold mine up. "I think they're lovely."

She squints at the keys. "If I can find metallic paint," she says, "absolutely." She smiles. "That's actually a very good idea, Peri." She elbows me, saying, "You're good that way."

I wish I *felt* "good that way" more often, but I'm okay to just enjoy the feeling right now. I smile happily at my feet as we trudge up the trail Ull is leading us on.

"Look," Ull gasps stopping in his tracks. We stand on tiptoe to see over his shoulders, to see what he's pointing at. A small squirrel is stopped in its tracks and is staring at us, too. It twitches its tail curiously. Then it creeps forward slowly.

Of course, this isn't normal squirrel behavior at all. It sniffs the air, then sits up and looks at us all again.

"Hi little guy," Ull says. He waves just a little bit. The squirrel twitches its tail again. That's when a tree frog calls and the squirrel darts away.

"Is it just me," Wink asks, "or have you heard a lot more tree frogs lately?"

I shake my head. "I thought tree frogs only lived in the rainforest until you told me otherwise-- I wouldn't have been paying attention until now."

Ull thinks back. "In regards to the symphony of the forest," he says, "they did seem to have a new arrangement in which the tree frog section carried the melody more strongly."

We decide to pretend that there was nothing odd about that sentence.

"I wonder," Wink says and then she pales. "Guys?"

Ull and I look at her confusedly, waiting for an explanation. She shivers, though it's not so cold now. "I don't know," she murmurs, "but I have a bad feeling."

Part of me, a small part, scoffs. A bad feeling-- just the one? That's nothing, of course. I have leagues of them, assailing on all sides, most of the time. Part of me wants to feel superior, somehow, for this-- but, of course, that doesn't make sense at all.

"What…. Sort… of bad feeling?" I ask   slowly.

She is gripping her key so tightly that her knuckles are white. "I don't know," she says, slowly. She shivers. "I've never felt like this before, exactly…" She glances around. "Are the tree frogs getting louder?"

They are. It sounds as though a tree frog army is surrounding us and their chirps are growing ever louder. Ull covers his ears and gives a little jump and squeak. I blink at him in surprise, then turn to Wink. She is shuddering and shivering; I've never seen her like this at all. Yes, the tree frogs are loud, but why are they affecting Ull and Wink like this? I touch Wink's shoulder lightly. "Wink?" She jerks away.

Now the sound is getting to me too. My very vertebrae are rattling with the sounds of chirping tree frogs. My heart beats hard at a different beat from the chirps. It's maddening. I glance around, but don't see any frogs. "Wink," I say, speaking loudly in a futile attempt to speak over the frogs-- "Wink, are you sure these are tree frogs? Ull, was ANYTHING ELSE brought from the magic world to ours?"

Wink just yelps. Ull is on the ground covering his ears now. "Ull," I plead, crouching close to him. "Please."

He's clearly not going to answer me anytime soon. And Wink is out for the count, too. I stand up, glancing around--wincing, wondering if we could possibly pass out and just not have to deal--

and that's when something small and sharp pricks my cheek. I cry out, jumping. Then I huddle to the ground like Wink and Ull are.

To my shock, my eyes slowly focus in on a very miniscule person approaching me. It looks like a tiny barbarian lady. Part of me, possibly a hysterical part, is tempted to laugh. She can't be more than two inches tall. She is dressed in furs-- my brain tells me mouse and squirrel skins, though I'm not sure how I know this. Probably because sometimes I just know things.The person is holding a very sharp twig, clutched tightly in her left hand. She has very dirty, very tangled hair. She opens her mouth and cries that sharp, loud cry.

"Stop it," I say. "You're hurting my friends." I feel oddly calm, as though I'm in control of the situation (I'm totally not). I guess after seeing giants for so long, very small people don't seem like anything all that exciting. In fact, it seems almost disappointing. I do not like this little person at all. And part of me does harbor love for the giants. It's hard not to love them and feel for them; their orange eyes are so sad and their lips always trembling. It occurs to me that they would be so wonderful smiling, and I feel the need to survive this and get the giants home as quickly as possible. To break the punishment, or curse, or whatever, and see them smiling widely.

"Then you stop," the tiny woman says, moodily.

I narrow my eyes. "Stop what?" I demand. "Who are you? Why are you mimicking the tree frogs?"

"Looks who's talkative," she says like that's a bad thing. Strangely, part of me takes this as a compliment. I've never been called talkative before, but I wish I had. I kind of like it. Maybe I would be talkative, if there were more people to talk to. Maybe I'd like people better if I knew more of them.

"You didn't answer the question," I say. The tree frog squeaks (which I know now weren't from tree frogs at all) have died down. I can hear Ull and Wink groaning.

"Questions, with an s," the tiny lady corrects me. Then she sighs. "I'm Ai, leader of the brownies."

Brownies, a little part of me squeals. *Giants and trolls and brownies!*

"Furthermore," she continues, "I am the finest tree frog breeder to ever exist. Possibly the first. But certainly the finest."

I try to look very impressed.

"And my people and I are mimicking the tree frogs because they disrupt your brainwaves. Or, they should," she says looking me over. "Your brainwaves must be made kind of funky."

I've never had my brainwaves insulted before and I'm a bit unsure of how to handle this particular situation. So I go for the next obvious question. "Why?"

She crosses her arms. "Because you're going to make us go *home* like in the *prophecy* and we *like* it right here where we are, thanks."

I'm surprised. "You don't want to go home?" I say with confusion. Then I think about my home and the quiet and how it doesn't truly feel like home. I wonder if it's the same thing.

She gets a funny look over her face-- and, oddly enough, she looks prettier made uncomfortable. I try to school my features to some sort of face that might encourage her to continue to let down her guard. Anything to keep the chirping down. I think I come off just looking... weird. But, at least I tried. Plus, she doesn't seem to notice or care very much. In fact, she just keeps talking as though she has wanted to say all of this to someone for ages. She probably *has*, I realize.

"At *home*," she says, "they might not even *miss* us. They probably don't even want us to come back. If they'd liked us, they wouldn't have left us behind when they *knew* the portal was closing. They'd have warned us." Her lip quivers though she tries to stop it, to look steely. "He'd have warned me," she mumbled, cheeks flushing a little bit.

I reach my pinkie finger out for her to shake. She seems to know what I'm going for, because she takes it in her small, suntanned hands and shakes it firmly. "I'm Peri," I say. "And the giants and trolls need to go home, but I won't make you go home. And," I say, dropping my voice lower. "I'm sure you're missed. Absence, you know, it makes the heart grow--"

"--Fungus," she finishes as I say "fonder." We look at each other in confusion, then laugh. "I like your version better," she says. Then her face goes stern again. "But we *must* go home if the portal opens. We'll be pulled into it. Everything magic will."

I hadn't known this. With a sinking feeling in the pit of my stomach, I realize that the pink-and-purple pine trees will be pulled in. It'll destroy the forest. It might destroy my home. The magic rocks will be pulled in, if they really are magic--and I'm confused. I remember Wink telling me that the rocks were magic, but she never said if they really were or why.

That's when I realize I am clutching something in my pocket, with the hand that wasn't being held in Ai's. I slowly pull my hand from my pocket.

I am holding the magic rock that Wink gave me. I rub my thumb over it, feeling the dust of it on my fingers. It flashes in the light like the magic keys do. It's covered in little flecks of metallic sediment. I glance at Ai. Her deep green eyes have grown wide.

She pushes her dreadlocks back--and it occurs to me that brownie dreadlocks are the most interesting thing I've ever contemplated.

"You have a magic rock," she murmurs. She swallows, her neck constricting. "No," she says. "We can't let you."

I gape at her. "But," I begin--

Then I hear the tree frogs louder than I've ever heard anything.

And I black out.

XXI.

I see wild colors--and I hear something, the snatches of some song--and I come to screaming, shaking, the idea of a grocery store fixed firmly in my mind for reasons known only to my subconscious.

"It's okay," I hear Wink calling. I open my eyes wide, blinking hard. I try to breathe calmly. "It's okay," she repeats. "We're just--"

"A bit tied up right now," Ull says. He laughs, sounding a bit unhinged.

He's an odd duck. Or, maybe he's a duck-billed platypus.

I shiver. "Why is it so cold?" I ask, realizing that I am leaned against the ground, my wrists and legs bound.

Ull giggles and doesn't stop for a long time. Finally, he slacks off some and Wink says, "Ull's losing it. We're in a cave. I think the brownies are leaving us to die."

I think of Ai's eyes--and I laugh, because, well, *Ai's eyes.*

"Oh, you've lost it too," Wink says, miserably.

I couldn't possibly explain the joke, I realize, after opening my mouth to do so. So I don't. "You saw the brownies?" I ask instead.

She sighs. "I could only make out snatches. You were talking to them. Why didn't you get as messed up by the tree frog cacophony?"

I remember what Ai told me. "I have funky brainwaves, I guess." Then I say, "Their leader didn't seem like she'd leave anyone to die. She seemed hurt and lonely and scared. But not cruel."

Ull giggles again.

"Really, Ull," I mutter. I wish I could see them, but they've positioned us all on our backs. I can vaguely hear Wink breathing.

Ull giggles again, then breathlessly says, "I can't *help* it, this just happens sometimes. That I'll admit," he collapses into giggles and squeaks again. I think I hear him writhing around on the ground a bit. "And I do it in rhymes."

Okay, still rhyming. So he must be doing okay, all things considered.

"I don't think they'd leave us to die," I say again. However, staring at the ceiling of the cave, I realize something.

I can *see.*

So we must be near an opening.

"We could probably get out, somehow," I say. "We must be near the entrance."

"Or *exit,"* Ull corrects me. "Oh, my goodness, that's funny."

I wonder if he always giggles manically in dangerous and depressing situations.

I wiggle around. "We can make it," I say. "If I can just loosen these... rope things a bit." They don't exactly feel like ropes, but I can't tell what they must be. Vines seems too cliche. They couldn't possibly be vines.

I wiggle and I wriggle. I barely get a few minutes into my attempt when I realize it's futile. Or, I decide it's futile. Or, I feel that it's futile. It doesn't matter. It's futile.

I can just feel it.

Sometimes... I just know things.

Then I hear a little shout--almost a summons. I wriggle a little bit more because I can't help myself.

"Hey," a tiny voice calls, coming closer-- and I hear small footsteps. A young brownie boy suddenly is standing on my chest, and I must crane my neck to see him. He has a smattering of bright freckles across his face, and very curly, very dark hair. He grins. "I'm supposed to let you go but make it seem like you just escaped," he tells me. "Aunt Ai really wants to go home, though she can't say it." He shrugs, and then says with a seriousness that seems much older than he could be, "It's politics."

I nod. "Tell her I said thank you," I tell him. "That we all say thanks."

He grins a crooked grin and I see that he has a gap between his teeth. He nods. Then he sets about freeing us from the ropes, sawing at them with a miniscule knife, and arranging them to look broken. "Run," he tells us. Then he salutes me. "Go bravely."

Wink and Ull and I are stretching, but we pause when he says this. We salute him back.

I like that, I think. *Go Bravely.* I can feel it in my chest.

Wink grabs my hand as we step out. "Peri, I don't know how long we were knocked out. We could've lost a day. My mom will be so worried."

Ull and I exchange panicked glances. How far off course are we? Should we just head home now? Can we do that?

"Return," Ull murmurs, his voice cracking.

We glance up at the sky, all three of us. The sun is high in the sky now--it's either been a couple of hours or a full day. Maybe more. And we don't know where we are.

Soon I realize that Wink and Ull are both looking at me for a decision.

I'm a bit delighted, and then it sinks in that I should not be making any decisions. At all. It will be the wrong one, and I will screw it up because it's inevitable. Maybe that should be freeing because, well, if you screw up either way, it doesn't matter. But it's not freeing.

I am more scared right now than I was tied up in a cave or being attacked by tree frogs.

I glance around, and, my goodness, has the sun always been so bright?

"Peri?" Wink says.

I do not want to talk to her.

I want to get knocked out by the tree frogs again, I think. Oh, please, can't I just get knocked out?

And suddenly… I feel it. The breath of a giant. So wistful, cold, and foreboding.

This is all too easy. And it's stupid. The stupid satyress could've done something different than banishing giants to our world. And why would she do that? And why do I have to be involved? Ull's parents would be better. Or my parents. Even just Wink and Ull could complete it. I can't read the map, I can't escape from the cave, I can't make a decision.

That's when the decision hits me like a sledgehammer in the stomach, if a sledgehammer in the stomach could be almost relieving.

I'm done.

Yes, I'm done.

Just, in general. With all of it.

So, I just turn around and start walking.

"Peri!" Ull calls, a note of desperation in his tone. "Peri, where are you going?"

Yes, no, I'm done. There are no responses. That's too much effort. Furthermore, walking feels stupid.

Which is probably why I take off running.

XXII.

I crash through the forest, blood rushing in my ears. I'm sure the scenery is nice, but I don't care.

Like I said, I'm done.

I stop when I reach a small waterfall--also known as, simply, a stream gushing quite suddenly from a rockier part of the mountain face. And, in that moment, I can picture the entire rock face crumbling, crumbling, crumbling down on me. I jerk away, but I stumble as I do and fall down. I feel my palms scrape, and I wonder if I should have brought antibiotic cream in my bag since scrapes can get infected. Then I picture Ull shaking his head and shuddering because *doesn't it feel wrong?* And I'm glad I didn't bring it. Then I remember that I ran away from him and from Wink, and I start crying.

I curl up as tightly as I can, fetal position. I haven't even really properly started crying when I can hear the quietest sigh of a giant. I sit up a bit, knowing my face is all dirty and red. I look up.

There is a giant, looking at me with utmost concern. He cocks his head, blinking his big, orange eyes at me, questioningly. I feel as though he is asking me if I am okay.

I open my mouth to say, "Don't worry, I'm fine." What tumbles out, like the water from the side of the mountain, is something else entirely. "I am so, so tired."

The giant nods, a tiny bit.

And it hits me.

He's communicating, just a tiny bit.

And I realize-- I have been communicating with the giants all along, in small ways.

I smile at him, shyly. "Hello, Mr. Giant," I say, with deeper respect than I have ever held for the giants before.

He sighs, but it's a pleasanter sigh than I have ever heard from any of the giants before now. He smiles a slightly crooked smile, shifting a bit. He blinks his orange eyes. Then he waves a tiny wave, one pinkie lifted in my direction.

It seems to take everything out of him. That's when I know that the giants are so, so tired too. And lonely. And I wonder, are the giants and I actually in the same boat?

I sit there, somewhat enjoying this mutual despair. My whole body feels too heavy and sore to move again, even though I'm kind of in an uncomfortable position. I regard the giant, but even regarding is exhausting. The mountain spring, or baby waterfall, or whatever I want to call it sings softly, and it sounds like--- like something I can't quite put my finger on. It's something nice, though. Apprehension tickles the corners of my mind, bringing a queasy feeling into the pit of my stomach. But my eyelids lower. I look up at the giant one last time. He is asleep.

And then, so am I.

"Peri!" It's a desperate voice, one I recognize; or, one I could recognize, if I wanted to put effort into it (which I don't). "Peri, please, what is going on with you?"

A lot of things, all the time, I think. This strikes me as funny, although maybe it isn't.

I realize my eyes are closed--I'm asleep. I try to move, to open my eyes, to sit up, but I can't seem to. It's like sleep is holding me back, trying to protect me from something. Or like it's holding me down, trying to suffocate me. Is it good, is it evil? What are its intentions? I struggle, for a moment, and then sit up, wide awake, heart beating very quickly, as though it's trying to prove to me that I'm still alive. Sleep paralysis. It's not my first time, but it's my first time in a long time. I had forgotten how awful it was.

"Peri!" I realize it's Wink and I feel half-guilty for some half-remembered dream where I was half-ignoring her. Or, was I? It's gone, whatever it was.

"Our fearless leader!" Ull declares. "So it wasn't an enchanted sleep after all! Or it was, but a minor enchantment-- one that is small."

"Not fearless," I mumble, pushing off Wink's embrace and standing up shakily. I brush pine needles and dirt off of me. I blink slowly. "Oh, no," I say, a horrible realization pouring over me. "How long has it been? How far off course are we? I never decided-- I just left--"

And surely, they must hate me now.

Ull's eyes are lit up, but only half with confusion and worry. Mostly, the other 50%, or maybe it's actually 51%, is lit up with excitement. "Peri, we're *really almost there.* You ran the right way! How did you know?"

I didn't, of course, but I can't get words to come out. *I didn't mess anything up.* I grin. "I didn't," I laugh. *Maybe I am a good leader.* "I just went."

"Well done," Ull tells me. "It's good to be able to just go."

It *is.* And I hope Wink is proud of me, too.

The giant, Mr. Giant, isn't here anymore. I don't know when he left. I wonder where he went. Maybe he's taking a nap now-- somewhere. I don't know where the giants live.

But I do know where they should live.

And we're almost there.

But, first things first.

"Okay," I say. "Now it is time to consult the map. Ull, will you do the honors?"

He grins, and pulls it from his bag. Unrolling it, he rubs his thumbs against it. "I bet you can guess where to go, ladies."

We bet we can, too.

His silver eyes dance. "North. North and we're nearly there."

XXIII.

North, and we're nearly there.

It's late afternoon, and we have long since run out of food. Wink and I should've been headed back home ages ago. I don't even know where home is from here. I try not to think about that too hard because it isn't the task at hand. I remember Wink's mom saying that one time: "It is important to pay attention to the task at hand. The other tasks can wait to be dealt with." She had brushed flour off of her hands and turned to me, smiling. "You'll figure it out someday."

Today's the day!

Wink and Ull are discussing books. He's begging us to smuggle human books to him, "through the bridge," when he's "practicing keeping the bridges." Then he looks a bit wistful. "I'll have to find some way to enjoy it, anyways."

"I thought you wanted to be, like, a bard," I say, confused.

He and Wink exchange a glance, and I realize that I must've missed something when I… when I was indisposed.

"It's not realistic," he says finally.

This strikes me as ridiculous, a troll saying that a music career isn't realistic. "You're from a magical world," I tell him.

He shakes his head. "I'm not from a magical world, I'm just from a different world." He grins cockily. "But difficulty makes us strong. At least, that's what I tell myself, when I'm having trouble coping."

"Maybe I should try that one," I laugh.

Wink taps my shoulder. "What are you coping with?" She cocks her head, messy hair falling in her face. The golden hour sunlight catches her eyelashes. I turn to look at Ull. Silver in the golden hour is beautiful.

I look back at Wink. I shrug. "Existence, you know, the usual." I really don't know. I laugh, and say as much.

Time to go back to the original subject. "You'd be an amazing bard," I say to Ull.

He shrugs. "I don't know," he says. "Probably."

It goes very quiet; I think he's thinking. Wink and I look at each other. We don't want Ull to be sad. Not in the golden hour when everything is picture-perfect. I decide to distract him by bringing his attention back to his beloved map.

"What are we looking for?" I ask. "Can the map tell us?"

Ull looks down at the map. "Just one thing now," he says.

Wink cocks her head. "What is it?" She sounds tired; adventuring is harder than we thought it would be. But I think we like it.

He points a little ways in the distance to a large, cracked monolithic stone. "There."

Wink and I gasp nearly simultaneously. You see, this means it's *over*. We've *done* it.

Are we delighted or heartbroken?

I think we're delighted. We've done it! *I've done it.* We have been very brave. We have been braver than brave. We have been doubly-brave. *I* have been doubly-brave.

I squint at the rock. "What are the keys for?" I am imagining the staff being hidden in the crack and us simply pulling it out and commanding it to open the door.

Ull scratches his head, then tugs at a few locks of his silver hair. "Answer uncertain," he mumbles. Then he says something about "ascertain" and "assertion," but so quietly we can't fully understand it. He spins in a circle, then turns a semicircle, then jumps back to approximately his original position. "Alright," he says, rolling the map back up. He slides it over his shoulder and into his backpack. "We're going to do this." He fidgets. "I'm glad to be saving the giants,and helping Ai and my parents, of course," he says in a rush. "I just don't want to go." He casts his eyes my way. "I'd miss you two."

"I promised we'd visit," Wink reminds him.

"And we'll bring you so many books," I tell him.

He squeaks a little bit, then takes off running for the monolith.

"He's crazy," Wink and I say at the same time. Then, once again in perfect sync, "He's afraid."

We stare at each other. Sometimes we both just know things. We look back at Ull, who is practically to the monolith now.

"He doesn't want to lose his nerve," I say. "He's afraid he'll want to stay here forever."

"He couldn't of course," Wink says. "Circumstances. He's silver."

I try to run through scenarios. We could paint him up. But *every day?* And what if he got wet? We could try to find a magic way. But should you really change who you are like that? What you're made to be?

"It's not really here he wants, anyways," she says to me conspiratorially. "It's rhymes, that's what he wants, isn't it?"

"Freedom," I nod, realizing that she's right. And I think about what he said to me, earlier, *"and you would be brilliant, were circumstances ideal."* He would be brilliant, were circumstances ideal. Then I wonder--why can't circumstances be ideal? Are any circumstances ideal? How do we know that these aren't the ideal circumstances for brilliance?

And I want to run, run up to the blue sky, breathe in the sky, and promise him that we will both be brilliant-- aren't the circumstances what we make them? Aren't we brave? Haven't we nearly saved the giants?

I suppose it would be more impressive if we saved the giants.

I take Wink's hand. "We can do this," I say mostly to myself.

She squeezes my hand. "I needed that," she says. I am surprised. I hadn't thought of her as ever needing encouragement. I figured that Wink was always confident, always sure, always feeling brave.

And I've always wanted to be like that.

She tugs my hand and we head up the mountain.

The earth is an interesting thing, to have mountains like it does. Part of the ground decided to raise itself up, separate from and yet connected to the rest of the ground. It looks like you should just be able to run up them, but you can't; your legs will burn. Your tendons grow tight. And, if you've already been hiking---running--exhausted all day, it's twice as bad. Ull made it look so easy; I suppose he must be built differently from humans, seeing as he's a troll. Maybe running uphill is easier for trolls. If I were scientifically inclined, this would interest me more. However, I am myself; therefore, I am only mildly interested.

We reach the top, and we see that Ull is peering inside of the crack. "There's a little *door,*" he whispers. "I don't know what it's for!"

Maybe it's for possibilities, some small voice in my head whispers. Maybe it's for whatever circumstances deem it needs to be.

I shake myself from the abstract, and Wink and I release each others' hands to climb the monolith and join Ull, to peer into the monolith's crack and reach to touch the door for possibilities.

It *is* a little door. It's a little yellow door, round, made of wood. Like in *The Hobbit.* I look at Wink, and she smiles, and I know she's thinking the same thing. We both smile. She's good like that, you know?

We're good like that, you know?

Ull is running his fingers over the small wooden door-- it's only big enough that he could reach his fist through it, were it to open. He gasps in delight. "The paint is chipping perfectly," he says.

"Perfectly for what?" I ask softly, so as not to disturb the moment.

"Perfectly for everything," he sighs, closing his eyes blissfully. "Perfectly. Like," he runs his tongue over his teeth a bit. "It's just *right.*"

We let him have his moment. Then he pulls out his key.

"It only has one keyhole," I say. "Why are there three keys?"

None of us know. None of us are sure. None of us moves to try to figure it out.

"Are we sure we want to do this?" Ull whispers.

Of course we are. "Of course we are," I say, out loud. "Think of Ai."

"Yes, think of Ai. What was it she said, that they might not even miss her?" Wink says heatedly. Too loudly.

"Think of--" I'd been going to say, *the Trolls,* but I catch Ull's expression. He doesn't want to go back because he's never been there. He was born here. You can't miss what you've never known, they say. I'm not sure that's it, though. You can't miss what you don't want at all. Only his parents want it. I swallow hard. "Think of the giants."

Ull and Wink don't speak or move.

"Think of the giants," I say again. "We promised we'd do this. They need this. They're ready for this. They've waited long enough." When Wink and Ull remain silent still, I feel heat rising in my face. *"I promised the giants,"* I say, and though it's a whisper, it feels more dangerous than had I screamed it with the rage of a thousand stars. "I promised them. They need to go home. Think of home. Think of home," I say, but as I say it, I realize that I don't even know what I mean. I'm all mixed up. How can I tell them to think of home, to convince them, when I hate home so much? When home doesn't feel like home? When the closest to home I have ever, ever felt was in this forest for the past day. Yes, despite the danger. Yes, despite the fear. Yes, despite my own feelings. The adventure felt like home. Wink and Ull felt like home.

Now, I don't want to unlock the door, ever. That would mean it was over. Circumstances, of course.

Although, changing circumstances would allow for new modes of brilliance. New experiences.

Maybe even for more home.

"We can do it," I say. "We need to. And it will be okay, somehow." I look up at Wink and Ull.

They nod.

Sometimes, we just know things.

And we will figure it out.

XXIV.

Ull's key unlocks the door. We don't hold our breath while he is unlocking it and opening, though part of me feels like we should. We should or else it's some sort of blasphemous. But we don't. We watch, and we breathe, and we wait.

It's over too quickly. It isn't like I'd imagined-- there's no bright glimmer of light, no angelic chorus, no rush of air to let us know if we've done the right thing or not. The door simply opens with a slight creak, like any door might. We peer in. There's some sort of small locked box inside, a small chest.

Ull pulls it out, and his hands shake a little. The box is wooden, too, and I think about Ull saying plastic just felt wrong. I think I can see what he meant now. If the box had been plastic, I would've hated it. It would've felt fake. This, this feels wholesome, natural, real. So, so incredibly real.

We try my key on the box. It doesn't unlock it. Wink's does.

I'm last, again-- except…

There's nothing to unlock.

Simply a faded piece of paper.

"North. You're nearly there." That's what it says. Ull, on a whim, turns it over. "You've probably been protected thus far. It gets harder from here. Leave your talismans behind."

"We don't have any talismans," Wink says.

I am already dropping my magic rock in the box.

Wink gapes in surprise, then demands to know how long I've had the rock in my pocket. "I don't know," I say. "It just appeared with the brownies. With Ai." I am struck with a feeling. "Check your pocket."

She shoves her hands in the pockets of her shorts. Her eyes grow wide. "It's…"

She pulls her magic rock from her left pocket. "I didn't put it there," she murmurs. "I promise you, I didn't."

I glance at Ull. He raises his hands as if to say, "Who, me?" Out loud he says, "I didn't bring protection. It hadn't occurred to me that we'd need it."

We make him check his pockets anyways. Nothing. He smiles widely. "I *told* you," he says. "You two must've known it'd be dangerous." How could we have known? "I never would've suspected danger," he laughs.

How could he not have?

We glance northward. We have all become well, well acquainted with the direction.

"Should we?" My lips form the words, but there is no sound. I glance at Wink, wondering, is she not ready to go home? Does she not need to go home? Does she not… want… to go home?

She grabs my hand, pulling. "We're almost there, Peri. We need to do this. You promised. You promised the giants."

I did promise the giants.

I grab Ull's hand. We are a chain. "Forward march?" I ask.

They nod.

We start walking north again.

I feel a slight tremor of worry at the thought of more danger. If what we've experienced so far has been safe and protected, well, then, danger isn't going to be my favorite. However, I am a bit glad that it isn't over, not quite yet.

I do wonder-- are Wink's parents worried? Are Ull's?

I know mine aren't.

No one worries about me.

Well, maybe that's not entirely true. Occasionally I worry about myself. And maybe the giants worry, sometimes, too. But, other than that-- I don't think anyone does.

The phone is probably still at home, hanging silently.

Ring, ring ring.

"What was that?" I ask cautiously. At this point, it could be my mind playing tricks on me…. Or it could be magic playing tricks on me.

"I think it's my… my mom?" Wink says confusedly. She is glancing around, scratching the back of her neck. She pushes hair out of her face, seeming flustered.

Ull blinks slowly. "But it's a *harmonica,*" he says. "Harmonicas don't sound anything like a mom. And the sound has been here all along."

Wink and I must look confused-- and we are confused-- because he explains. "Since we started off yesterday, the harmonica sound has been following us. So what if it's a bit louder now?" He laughs. I think he laughs when he's afraid. I think he's scared right now.

Like I am. Because I can still hear it.

Ring, ring, ring.

It's not a harmonica. It can't be. It's a *telephone.*

"Okay," I say, taking a deep breath. "This must be what the rocks had been protecting us from. Sounds." It sounds ridiculous even as I say it and know that, somehow, it must be true. Maybe there's part of it that I am missing, yes, but this is at least a part of the truth. "Think, what could the sound do to us?"

"Well, my mom's voice would make me worry that I needed to get back home," Wink says. "It *does*. It makes me worry that all of this is over. And, I probably do need to get back home. But, Peri, you haven't told us what you're hearing."

I blush. I don't want to admit it. It feels like to explain would make me naked, put me in danger. But, looking at Wink and Ull, and seeing that they have told me what they hear, I know I really can't avoid it. Especially, especially if I've become the leader, somehow. So I admit. "I, well, I hear the telephone."

Wink raises her eyebrows. "Peri?"

"Which is ridiculous," I continue over her, "because the phone hardly ever rings at my house. Not that it bothers me, of course. It's ridiculous that I'd be hearing this, since I don't *really* care. And if I do care, I shouldn't," I can't seem to stop talking. I cover my mouth with my hands.

"Peri," Wink says, "you always get so excited when your parents-- and, if I hear my mom calling me, maybe you're hearing *your* parents calling you--"

"Maybe I'm missing the call," I mumble through my hands. It feels as though I have been splashed with freezing water. "They're calling and I'm missing it."

Wink shakes her head. "I don't know," she says, "I think... because, Ull is being called by a harmonica."

Ull speaks up, next. "Maybe it's more that what we don't want to call us is calling us."

"You don't want the harmonica to call you?" Wink asks pointedly.

He flushes, and I wonder how even his blush is silver, when it could-- and maybe should-- be copper. "Well," he allows, "it's complicated, of course."

Wink and I don't have to say we agree. Of course we agree. I very badly want my parents to be calling me; It's just that, for some reason, I also don't.

"Why a harmonica?" I ask after we have been leaning against the trees in silence for too long listening to the noises.

"Oh," he says. "My dad found a harmonica out by our house once. Said it was pollution. But, I had heard the person who had left it playing it." He gets a funny look in his eye. "I couldn't entirely understand *that* language."

That's lovely, I think, but don't say. Because it isn't just lovely. It's also sad. So, so sad.

Ring ring ring.

"We should keep going," I say.

I wish, the tiniest, softest, innermost wish that they didn't follow me when I said that.

But, of course… They do.

I wanted for so long to be in charge for once, but, now that I am, I kind of can't wait for things to go back to normal. For Wink to be in charge. Because, now, she's still the brave one. She's just not the leader.

The forest feels too quiet up here. Except for the noises. Those are getting louder. The ringing is nearly maddening, and I'm just trying to ignore it. And I don't know how far from home we are or why Ull has quit using the map. I'm just going where I feel that we should be going. That's what scares me most of all. My feelings are so unpredictable and they're usually wrong.

That's why I'm relieved when Wink says, "We aren't headed north, now, we're headed northwest."

Deep breath. "Can you reorient us?"

She obliges.

"Ull," I say, "do you want to check the map?"

He shakes his head moodily. "Can't you tell that the sounds are getting louder? I think that means we're nearly there. They're trying to turn us back."

I squint at him because how does he know? He can't know. But he seems to. But, is it a feeling he's having that may or may not be wrong? Furthermore, why am I trusting Wink's sense of direction? If I can't trust hers, or mine, or his, then whose direction *can* I trust, and how can I go anywhere?

"Peri?"

I shush Wink. She recoils like I might've slapped her, or something.

I reach my hand out towards her, frightened. "I'm sorry, Wink," I say, but she just steps a bit closer to Ull.

They're more together than they're with you, a little voice in my head whispers.

That's when it occurs to me that this voice is not my voice. It's an evil-sounding voice. And the ringing, the ringing, the ringing is getting louder.

"Wink?" I say softly, "there's a voice in my head."

Ull speaks before she does. "I do *not* hate tradition," he says and he squeezes his eyes closed. "Goodness, you're loud. How can you possibly play the harmonica and talk at the same time?"

He isn't talking to me. I think he must also be talking to the voice and to the sounds.

Ring, ring, ring. Ring, ring, ringringring.

Nobody ever worries about you.

Wink is crying, I realize, with a start. I don't see her cry often. When I do, I usually look away. Now, though, I have a different thought. And it's my voice, quiet under the ringing and the hateful, hateful mumbling. *When I'm scared, or sad, I stare at the phone waiting for it to ring, for someone to notice me and help me. But I don't help Wink when she is sad.*

Ignoring the racket in my head, I step towards her. Suddenly, gravity feels dizzyingly strong. Black and white moves in my peripheral vision as the ringing *screams* at me. But I step again and

I collapse into some sort of hug for Wink. "Ull," I say--and I can't tell at what volume I am speaking-- "Ull, it's okay, come here."

I'm pretty sure he crawls towards us, but I can't tell. Every new *ring* is like an explosion. When I do think I feel his shoulders against ours, I do my best to include him in the hug.

Ring-ring-ring-ring.

Nobody even cares about you, and you can't do this. Of course you can't; how could you think you were capable?

"I'm so, so tired," I mumble into Wink's hair.

"I am too," I think I hear her say. I think I can hear Ull concurring, also.

"I've been tired," I add even more softly. "I just didn't want to say it."

With that admittance, I can breathe again. "It's very hard," I say, trying to speak louder over the still-ringing and still-calling voices. "It's very hard, because I am so alone so much of the time, and I don't know why even my parents don't love me enough to be there." I run the words together so quickly I'm not sure they can be understood as English. I swallow a breath when it's out, and, maybe for the first time ever, I feel actually brave.

And the ringing has stopped.

I sit up, straighter. I can see now, too, and the world seems too still and calm after the chaos that had so recently enveloped me. I look at Wink, who is curled up tightly, looking smaller than I had ever imagined she could be. Tears streaming down her face, silently. Too much noise within for noise to escape without. "Wink," I say, gently, "what's scaring you?"

She shakes her head.

"You can tell me," I say. I sound and feel calmer than I even expect myself to be. I look at Ull and tell him the same.

I am not really surprised when he speaks first. After all, he told us his fears after the cave. He told us his dreams. He told us his rhymes. He told us so much, so easily, so readily.

"I'm afraid," he says with odd confidence, "that no one will be proud of me." Then he leans back, mouth open wide, eyes closed. He runs his tongue over his teeth. Then he sighs and looks me in the eye. "If that's all it took to shut the noise up, then I feel stupid for not having just said it before." He shrugs. "But at least it's not loud, not anymore."

Part of me is shocked by how easy that was for him; part of me isn't, because he is himself.

Now we are both encouraging Wink, pleading with her, begging her lips to reveal more than silent sobs.

She will not reveal; her soul is guarded. I understand that, but I don't know what to do with it. Is that despair creeping back in?

No. No, it's not, because we are not alone. And Ull knows what to do. He runs his tongue over his teeth again before speaking. "Well, do the humans have the story of Aldebaran?"

"I represents the bear," I say quickly. Then I pause, wondering how long I've had this information. "It's a star in the constellation Taurus," I add mumbly.

Ull squints at me. "I don't know of this constellation," he says. "Interesting, that you say bear, though." He gets a funny look on his face, in his eyes. It occurs to me that this is his area, that he knows what he's doing right now. And I trust him.

"Aldeberan," he says, "was a young boy when he ventured out into the forest at night. The pink-and-purple pine trees swayed darkly, silhouetted against the golden moon. He tiptoed through the twisting trails, wandering. He whistled, and a wise owl called back."

It's like listening to the greatest bedtime story ever; it has been ages since I heard a bedtime story. I hadn't realized how much I missed them. I smile a little bit, and Ull seems to take this as the greatest possible encouragement. He continues with some sort of magical air around him--but not because he's a troll. Because he's sharing and because he's himself. Wink seems a tiny bit calmer, but still very quiet. She is hugging me tightly now. Part of me loves this hug. Part of me hates it, because I know she's been sad.

"He creeped, the young Aldeberan, until he came to the Magic Circle. Now, the Magic Circle was where the dryads played in the daytime. At night, though, it was empty. Abandoned. And full of lonely magic."

I can't help myself. "What's lonely magic?"

He cocks his head a bit, looking deep into my eyes. "Lonely magic is what happens when magic wanders listlessly until it finds someone in need of it. Someone alone. Someone hurting. And it tries to help them." He shrugs. "That's what magic is for, after all. Helping."

This sends chills down my spine. I think of Mr. Giant. I squeeze Wink tighter. I didn't know she could ever be *lonely* or *hurting*. I wish I'd been there for her, and then I am filled with resolve to be there for her more starting here and now, in these pine needles, on this mountain, in this forest.

"Aldeberan was a fearless boy, so he entered the circle. That was when the great Bull-King Taurus came."

That's the star Aldeberan's constellation, I think. Coincidence? Or Creation? I lean towards the latter.

"Taurus looked at Aldeberan. He saw a young, innocent boy. But, peering through the veils of time, he saw a brave, generous young man. And he said, looking at Aldeberan with piercing red eyes, 'I will give you power on this day.' Aldeberan didn't know what that meant, exactly, but he knew that Taurus was a good king. So, he nodded. Taurus smiled and spoke again. 'For as long as you are able to face your fears, you will have the power of the bear. You will call upon them, and they shall aid you. You shall become one in times of need. Their companionship is yours, boy. But, remember-- fleeing from fears will only harm you.' Aldeberan understood this, despite his child's years, his young perspective."

Ull himself sounds like he understands more than his young perspective should allow, right now. Wink's breathing is slowing back to normal, though she does occasionally give a small gasp.

"Aldeberan could, indeed, use all of the powers Taurus spoke of after this came to pass. Many brave feats he accomplished, many wild adventures he went on-- always returning to home, to family, to peace. Each time he went on an adventure, or went out questing, he uncovered some fear he had, and he faced it, with help. One night, however, when he was quite grown-up, he didn't come home. It grew very dark, and still, he had not turned up. It was well past his appointed time of return. His wife watched the clock ticking and ticking away. Finally, she stood up. 'No doubt some harm has befallen him,' she said. She tucked her children in, kissed them, and promised with no doubt in her mind that she would be back the next morning."

This is a foreign concept to me-- returning the next morning. Kisses. Children being tucked in. I am enthralled. I also have a sense of foreboding, for Aldeberan and his wife. "I hope she's okay," Wink whispers to me; it is the first she's spoken since the noise became unbearable. I search her face, wondering if her chaos is abating.

"Aldeberan's wife crept through the trees, clutching her bow. She had a sling of arrows on her back. She had no fear of using them, only of what she might have to use them on. Anyone or anything that could delay the bear Aldeberan must, surely, be a force to be reckoned with. Anyone or anything that could answer to Alderberan's wife after hurting him; however, that would truly be a brave creature.

"Creeping, crawling, crying silently, she searched. It seemed that she had spent hours in the silverly, slippery trance of moonlight when she finally found him. He was lying by the weeping willow, near a deep pool, not unlike the pool we so recently dived into. She dashed to his side. She demanded answers. She kissed him. Aldeberan simply looked up at her, something unfamiliar in his eyes. It took her a few moments to realize-- it was fear. Aldeberan was scared.

"She begged him to tell her what had happened, and she took his head in her lap. He didn't speak much of it, but he told her only this: he had not done as he should have done. He was afraid to tell her more. In the moment that he was afraid to call for help, he lost his bear form."

Wink whimpers, and we both stare at Ull, waiting for explanation. What *had* Aldeberan done? Would he ever get his powers back? How badly was he hurt? Did he and his wife return safely to their children? *Please, were they back by morning?*

Ull doesn't answer these questions. He only sighs. "And I shall let you draw your own conclusions."

What kind of storyteller are you? I want to demand, but something in me tells me that the answer is, *a pretty good one, actually.*

I can see it in his eyes. He's proud of his story, but he's mostly hoping for something. For some kind of response.

I think he gets it, because Wink shudders, and then says, "I do not want to be like Aldeberan when he lost his powers." She sits up, blinking at me tearfully. "Peri," she says, pleadingly, "you do like me, right?"

I answer easily. "You're my best friend. You're practically my sister. I love you."

She bites her lip, then speaks again. "But do you like me? My mom loves me, but I'm not sure she likes me."

Ull and I look at her as though the noise must've driven her insane. "Of course she likes you," I say, thinking of the times I have seen Wink's mom joking with her or calling her inside to see something interesting. "And she loves you. I do too."

Wink shifts. "Sometimes," she mumbles, "I'm afraid that I'm boring, that I'm just another McCall sibling."

I watch her face. The noise is going away for her now.

I wonder how she could ever think she was boring. She paints. She knows so much about tree frogs. She has the most amazing pinkie nail. And she believes in everyday magic. Sometimes, she just knows things.

She is anything but boring.

And everyone likes her, and most people love her, too.

I have always been jealous of her for all of that.

And... for the first time, I tell her so.

Ull watches. I'm not sure if he's watching with reverence, or watching with the intention of telling this story someday. Then I wonder if, for him, reverence *is* telling the story someday. And I like him and love him, too.

Wink cries into my shoulder some. I just let her, wondering if we can both be the brave one. Maybe we can all be the brave ones, this big-picture part of my mind wonders. I like that thought. Go bravely. *Be* bravely. I never would've thought to *be* bravely, until just now--maybe Ull's odd use of language is rubbing off on me. But, it has a different meaning altogether than simply "be brave." I like it. I want to write it down.

Reverence.

No time now, though.

We all stand up; unspoken agreement. We must keep going. We have survived this. We are stronger, already, although we are all so, so tired.

We must save the giants.

XXV.

I think, maybe, maybe we're all *good that way* right now. Or all the time. I'm thinking all of these pleasant thoughts, as we walk in the sunlight. Ull has pulled the map out again; whatever quarrel he had with it earlier seems to have been abandoned and they are reconciled.

Ull is smiling at it, grinning happily, and giggling every few seconds. It's like the map is telling him secrets about the world, funny secrets, little things. At some point, he shoves the map in front of my face. "The wind is blowing north, too," he laughs.

I don't see why I need the map to know this. I could tell just fine without the map. But, then I do squint at the map and notice that everything in the map right now LOOKS like the north, and looks like it's moving north. It also-- does it smell like the north? What does the north smell like? It seems to smell like deep greens and so many blues. I look at Ull, wondering if he smells colors all the time or if this is just the magic of the map. "Show Wink," I laugh.

She loves this. I think it means more to her, since she is an artist. I think it is deeper for her, the colors and the meanings and the feelings. She can feel the movement of them now.

Then Ull gives a little cry. "I got distracted! We missed something! Had I been focusing, we could've acted!"

He jumps back a few steps, then squints down at the ground. "See," he says, "see, we missed it."

I promise there is *nothing* there. Well, nothing that I can see, at least. However, after years of being the only one who could see the giants, and after seeing that he could read the map even when I couldn't, I am not about to question him.

It's just a spot on the ground; to me it doesn't look all that different from, well, the rest of the ground. "Ull," I say, "what is it?" it's covered in pine needles and brush, whatever it is. Or maybe it's invisible. Nothing will surprise me now.

He just slides the map into his backpack and gets down on his hands and knees, digging in the earth. Wink and I, unsure of what we're digging for, drop to our knees to help, too. I feel bad to be disturbing the earth from its slumber, but I know Ull wouldn't be doing this without a good reason. That's why I sink my fingers into the cool, musty earth, pulling through ages of decaying leaves, feeling it caking beneath my nails. I can smell it, the earth. I wonder how many worms are wriggling away from our clutches, deeper into their subterranean home. Wink seems loath to get her special pinkie nail dirty or damaged--I can understand this. After all, it is her art. She digs with one hand, her 'regular' hand. I think this is very cool, but I don't feel comfortable saying so.

I am just about to ask what we're looking for when I feel something different beneath my fingertips. It's wood, but not the musty, decaying, half-rotten wood we had been digging up. It is not soft, it is not wet. It is sturdy and flaking with paint-- it feels like the little round door guarding the place we had left our magic rocks in. Ull gasps and pulls his silver hands from the ground. They are dirty, very much so. He rubs the dirt up his arms a bit. It streaks like paint up his silvery arms. "This is it," he says.

It. A vague term, meaning nothing highly specific, but always used to indicate something highly specific. An interesting word. A great word. I love *it.* This strikes me as funny, but I am being reverent. Then I wonder if it is irreverent of laughter for me to not laugh, so I do allow myself a small smile. A laughing smile.

"This is what we missed," Ull says, pulling a small box from the ground. It is painted with the same peeling yellow paint of the small, round door. It is latched with a simple hook-and-eye. I have seen similar latches in the older buildings on Wink's family's property. It is not rusted, like those are; It is silver, almost like it is brand new. I look at Ull's fingertips, so close to it. They are nearly the same silver. Shiny. It's a gentle shine, though-- not an industrial shine. I think this would please Ull.

He slowly unlatches it, unhooks it, opens the lid. It creaks, ever so slightly, as though it is warning us half-heartedly that we may not want to do this. Of course, a half-hearted warning never stops questing. It won't stop us, not now.

Inside the box is a small leather-bound book. It is wrapped with a single small strand of leather, holding it closed. Ull gently removes the book from its box, and presses his lips against the cover.

"It's magical," Wink murmurs. I have to agree. I think, based on Ull's expression when he pulls back, that we have guessed correctly. This is a book laced with magic, touched with things unseen. Things I can't understand.

Reverence, I think again.

Then with a shiver down my back, it's beginning.

He opens the book. Gently, and squints at the yellowed pages. The pages are much thicker and rougher than any paper I am used to seeing; it must have been made by older processes, in older times. He runs his fingers across the page, and he squints at words that I can't make out. "It's..." he trails off.

"Some form of elvish, I can't read it," Wink says, referencing *Lord of the Rings.* I smile a laughing smile again-- reverence for the moment, reverence for the humor.

"It's not elvish," Ull says seriously. "Don't be ridiculous. It's Runic, the language of the satyrs."

Wink and I squeeze each other's hands tightly upon hearing this. I'm not sure when we found each other's hands behind Ull's back, but we did. I suppose it's the excitement of the moment pulling us closer. We've been like that since we were little. When we're excited, we're like magnets pulling close together to share in the fun.

Of course, it occurs to me that neither of us has been very excited for some time.

"Do you read Runic?" I ask hopefully.

Ull blushes a silvery blush. "I, um," he says, "I only sort of paid attention when my father was teaching me that." He glances at the ground around us. "It wasn't very interesting. Runic is the one language Trolls must learn. We speak all others naturally, but Runic is a higher tongue. I... I figured I'd never need to know it."

I want to admonish him, but my parents left me with a French book when they went away this last time. I promised I'd study it, but, as soon as they were out of the driveway, all motivation left me. I shoved the book under a couch cushion and went upstairs to take a nap. I have avoided that particular couch cushion ever since.

"Do you remember *anything?*" Wink pleads.

I hope he does. To go on not knowing-- or to turn around and head back to Mr. and Mrs. Troll-- seems abominable. I can't imagine really doing it.

Ull bites his lip and studies the paper seriously. "I think," he says, "I think it's 'the... something... of the satyress.' The root here goes back to what, in English, translates as *annual.* Or años, in Spanish." He blinks hard. "Why, why do I have to know Spanish?"

Maybe Ull should be my foreign languages tutor.

"So… so could it be *annals?*" I ask. "Like, you know, *the annals of the kings of Judah?*" I've read the entire Old Testament three times, but only made it through the New Testament once. "The Annals of the Satyress?"

Ull jumps up excited. "Yes," he cries, "Yes, that's it. This is the book of the Mystic!" He skips a few steps away from us, and he turns the page, pacing as he examines it. "Thank you for your etymology knowledge, Peri."

I don't really have any actual etymology knowledge. I push some hair behind my ear, feeling self-conscious.

"The giants," he reads slowly. He squints, skimming the pages. "Well," he says, "there's something here about… war crimes. Very trying times."

Wink steps a little closer to me. "War crimes?"

"I can't tell for sure," Ull says softly, "but it looks like the giants were at war." He looks up, eyes wide. "This would be why my parents just get sad and quiet when I ask what exactly the giants did."

I am having sudden second thoughts about saving the giants. I think of Mr. Giant. He didn't seem like a war criminal. He just seemed sad. He didn't seem like he would threaten peace-- other than the fact that his presence and the presence of his people has been threatening my peace for years. I guess I was always okay with that because I didn't have much peace to begin with.

But, the question is--is it right to allow those who couldn't live with each other to…. Go back to living with each other?

This feels like one of those big, deep questions I'd be asked to ponder after finishing a history book or a gripping novel. Or something that manages to be both genres. I don't want to consider it. It's like the French book; I want to hide it away, avoid it, shove it beneath the cushions. I want to go upstairs leaving it to its own devices.

Wink takes my hand. "Remember," she says, "when we first realized the giants needed saving. The truth of it is, they've learned their lesson. Of course they might forget it. They probably will. But that's what second and third and fourteen-billionth chances are for. It's for the hope of a better outcome."

I sigh. *Why? Why do we hope for a better outcome if people always fight and leave and hurt each other?*

Ull looks up. "I think I've made out enough," he says. He puts the book in my hands. I don't look down at the book, but I also don't look into his eyes. I sort of look past him, my fingers fumbling to hold the *Annals* together. "The Satyress, the Mystic, she knew that someday, it would be time for a return. Exiles don't last forever."

I don't say anything. I try to find the background noise of the forest, birds singing. I just hear the breathing of giants.

"It's time to return," Ull whispers in my ear, stepping between me and Wink. He starts smoothing the dirt where we were digging. He is packing it away, patching the hole we created.

"Peri?" Wink says. "Are you ready to return the giants to their home?"

Of course not! If we return them, what's to stop them fighting again?

A selfish voice in my head murmurs, *at least, Peri, at least they'll be separate from you. They may disrupt their whole world's peace, but not yours, not anymore.* I can't tell if this is my own voice or the evil voice from earlier. They sound a bit the same.

And, what about Ai? She wanted to go home. Who is the *he* she had mentioned? Is *he* still waiting for her? It was complicated, though. *Politics.* And the Trolls. Mr. and Mrs. Troll clearly wanted to go home, but wasn't Ull happier here?

Or, will Ull always feel out of place?

I glance at him. He's so serious in this moment. He always seems to be feeling one thing or another and feeling it quite deeply.

I don't want him to be sad, but I don't know what would keep him from being sad.

"Peri," Wink says again gently. She takes my hand. "Remember? The giants have been waiting for us to come and save them. It isn't good to be alone."

I know what she's saying is true. I also know that all of the things I'm thinking have truth, too.

I open the *Annals.* Of course, I can't read Runic, but I study the alien shapes anyways.

"Aw, Peri," Ull says, in a shockingly light tone, "do you want us to talk you into it?"

I look up at him, at Wink. "I don't want the giants to cause more pain. I don't want them to stay here, because they're sad and they make me sad." I see something flash in Wink's eyes. "They make us sad," I amend. "But, if we send them back home, and they cause more pain…"

Wink balls her fists. "Peri, you've been looking into the eyes of the giants longer than I have! How come you can't see that it's time? They're ready. They need each other! Or, maybe you can't see that because you're always too busy pretending that *you* don't need *anyone."*

I clutch the *Annals* more tightly, my fingernails digging into leather. Irreverence. Ull opens his mouth as though he might speak, but then bites his lip and retreats, eyes wide.

I try to speak levelly, but I know my voice betrays me. I look at the ground, trying not to cry. "I need everyone always, but no one ever comes." Then I throw the *Annals* at her feet. "Go save the giants," I say. "I don't want to anymore. I mean it this time."

I walk away, the *thump* of the *Annals* hitting the ground still echoing in my ears.

Yes, I thought I was done before, but--this time, this time, surely I do mean it.

XXVI.

This time, I don't go far. I don't run, either. I walk, stiffly, and I sit down only a few feet away from where I left Wink and Ull.

I think. I think so much that it feels like someone has doused my brain with water-- muddy water.

I don't want to save the giants anymore. And I know Wink takes that as betrayal. Like I'm abandoning her, not just the quest.

"I've been abandoned lots. She'll be fine," I mutter.

I hear a small, quiet voice whisper back to me, *Peri, Peri. Peri, child, you know better. In every book you've ever read, in every song you've ever sung, and every time you've looked in another being's eyes. You know better.*

I'm not just abandoning Wink. I'm not just abandoning the giants, or some abstract idea of a grand quest. I'm abandoning everything I've ever longed for, everything I've ever wished to become true.

But, of course, it's too late now.

"Peri?"

I jump up, startled.

It's Wink, standing behind me. She holds her hands out as if to say, *what is there to say?*

I don't mean to speak. But I do. "I really wanted to be the leader, but I'm doing an awful job of it, aren't I?" I sniffle. "And I was wrong. You come lots when I need you, but now you won't anymore. And I thought I was doing a good job!"

"Oh, *Peri.*" She sighs. "You're doing a very good job. Sometimes I think you spend so much time thinking about life that you wind up not really living life."

I flush. It feels like my soul is naked. Or, not exactly naked-- but in a swimsuit it's self-conscious in, for sure. "You live life well." Then I restate, "I've always been jealous of you, for that."

She looks like maybe her soul has been partially stripped down, too. She shakes her head. "Why?"
I shrug. I'm feeling done again. "You seem happy."

"Oh," she says. "I mean, I'm not always. Sometimes I'm really not, because... I feel like I'm just another sibling. But, even when I'm not happy, I've learned to be. I bet you could, too."

I didn't know how lost in the mix she felt. I wonder how I didn't see it before. I wonder why I haven't learned to be happy already. Then I remember what Ai said, about my brain waves being made funky. Maybe I can. Maybe it's just a bit harder for me. I remember that small voice, telling me I know better. I do.

"I'm really sorry, Wink," I say very softly. "I don't want to abandon you."

I don't feel like she quite grasps the gravity of that statement.

But she does help me up, and pulls me back to Ull, who is lying on his back in the middle of the forest, lazily flipping through the *Annals of the Satyress.* He looks up when we are near him. "Welcome back, ladies," he says, grinning. "Ready to go with no *if*s, *and*s, or *maybe*s?"

"That wasn't quite a rhyme," I tell him.

"Slant rhyme," he says, jumping up. "If your ears squint, it sounds like a rhyme."

127

Should I tell him your ears can't squint? I decide not to. I just laugh, smile. He's part of the *better* that I know. Wink squeezes my hand. She's part of the *better* too.

"Are we continuing the quest?" He asks. "I trust you two to make the decision that's best."

Wink whispers, "You're the leader, Peri. It is your call."

I'd prefer it to not be my call. But, it is mine--and I know what I am supposed to do.

I whisper, "Return."

Of course, it occurs to me how ambiguous this is. It could mean anything, really. Return home, return mail, return the gift....

Return the giants to the place they need to be.

Ull jumps up and presses the *Annals* into my hands. "Brilliant," he cries. "The quest goes on!"

He whips out his map, blushing when Wink wiggles her eyebrows as he gently unrolls it. "I love everything," he tells us, "and it's almost quite embarrassing."

We love him for loving everything, though. I think he realizes that.

"I know I said 'We're nearly there,' before," he laughs, "but this time, I promise. This time, I'm sure."

Although I had so recently panicked and declared that I didn't even want to save the giants, now I am ecstatic. I bounce a bit and squeal. Wink throws her arms around me. "We *did it,* or we will have!" she says.

Ull grins. "Now, let's go!"

XXVII.

Everything feels lighter, somehow, and braver, and more beautiful. The giants seem to be humming, not sighing--but, I can't hear them, so I don't know how I know this.

I'm pretty sure we have reached the peak, the zenith, the top. It's near dark. My legs are wobbly-tired. That's what Wink's youngest brother says, when he is sleepy. *He gets wobbly-tired.* That's definitely the proper terminology here. I glance over at Wink. I start to wonder if I should ask if she is also wobbly-tired, but then instead of wondering, I ask. "Are you wobbly-tired?"

She laughs, slumping against a tree. "I am so wobbly-tired." She grins. "I'm surprised you remembered that."

"Are you kidding? I love Miller," I tell her. "He's the sweetest."

"You can *have* him." She grins. "He's chaos toddling."

Ull purses his lips; he has stopped, also, and he is regarding us with confusion. "Who is Miller?"

"He's Wink's little brother," I say. "He's four, and he's the best. He says he gets wobbly-tired when he's sleepy."

"That's kind of like the English kenning but in a verb form," Ull says, eyes lighting up. "It's brilliant!"

I have no idea what he is talking about; one glance at Wink tells me she is also just as confused.

Ull is also chaos.

But then, after all, so am I.

"We're here, by the way," Ull says, casually, like this is no big deal at all. "We're here, at the end, for real."

I glance around. "But where's the cave? North Cave?" I remember him saying this, mentioning this earlier. There are no obvious caves.

"Ah," he says. "That would be a good question." He squints at the ground. He grins, silver cheeks shining in the dappled light of the trees. He suddenly slips the map into his backpack, and grabs my and Wink's hands. He starts tugging us, tugging us a little behind a cluster of thick, bushy firs.

And there it is.

A large monolith with a deep, deep pocket.

"That's not exactly a cave," I say.

"Don't be nitpicky," Ull sighs. "Someone named it North Cave, so, that's what it's named. I mean, I'm not a *return."*

But you are part *of the return,* I think. This makes me smile a little. I wonder if he sees it; if he will see it; when he will see it.

Ull steps toward the cave, then kind of dances backwards a few steps. He bows to me. "Lovely leader, take us to the start of the end."

I suppose that's when it hits me that it is no longer beginning. It hasn't been, not for a while now.

The end is beginning.

That means that it's ending.

I walk towards the cave, and walking feels very awkward and embarrassing. I glance over my shoulder; they aren't following me. They're just standing there and watching me, for some reason.

"Guys," I say, "come one. We're saving the giants."

That stirs them to life, and Wink runs to me, grabs my hand. Ull comes a moment behind and grabs my other hand. We're a team, now.

I can hear a warbler calling, somewhere in the distance. Those are the yellow birds, I remember--they have the sweetest, purest sound. They're my favorite birds ever. They're yellow, like the sun, like Wink's favorite flip-flops, like my mother's nicest shirt. I wonder what the birds sound like in the giants' world. I realize that I may never know. As we walk closer to the *not*-cave, I glance at Ull. Surely he will tell us. When he's helping run the bridges.

When we step foot into the rock--because it is stepping inside of the rock--I feel a shiver run down my back. The rock is old. Impossibly old. I can see so many layers, laid by floodwaters stronger than I can imagine. Ull, as if on cue, brushes his fingers against the rock face.

"A masterpiece," he says. Reverence. Then he grins at us. "You have your key, right, Peri?" When I nod, he grins more widely. "I believe we will need it."

I wish my key weren't last; but I'm also glad to be finishing it, since I started it. Sometimes I feel like I am always a little ahead or behind Wink. Mostly behind. She seems so grown-up and happy.

Maybe my brainwaves are funky.

Right now, though, I'm a little ahead of her. I'm taking a step, and I'm pulling her and Ull along behind me. "Come on," I say, and my voice bounces strangely off of the rock walls. "Come on, we're here! We're *saving the giants!*"

It's-ending, it's-ending, it's-ending, it's-ending.

132

In the very back of the 'cave,' there is a huge trunk. It looks a bit like the one that my mother takes with her whenever my parents leave, except that my mother's is covered in stickers from different places. This one is simply metal, wood, and dust. So, so much dust. This is the first relic-type thing we have seen that does not look perfectly new.

Wink draws a breath, deeply. "That's staff-sized," she says.

"Not a very full staff. You'd have to hope it was a slow day, or that some of them were working overtime."

Wink and I stare at Ull. A few seconds pass, and *then* we get the joke. I poke him with my key. "You, good sir," I say, "are the most ridiculous."

He beams. Then he looks at the chest again. "I can't wait to see it," he says. "I've only heard stories my whole life."

I also am itching to open it, which is why I don't take any time to appreciate the feeling of the rusty lock beneath my fingers as I fumble with the key. "Any minute now," I mumble, after it's already taken *way* longer than I would like.

"Are you sure you're doing it right?" Wink asks.

"No," I say honestly. "I'm really not."

Oddly enough, that's right when we hear a soft *click* and the lock falls. I let it hit the ground with a resounding metallic *clunk*. I feel excitement rising in me as the three of us work together to lift the lid, being careful of its sharp metal edges. We lean it back, slowly, propping it against the back wall of the 'cave.'

Within, there is only a long, thin object wrapped in linen. I lift it out, and Ull helps me slowly unwrap it. Wink stands back, appraisingly.

Wood, wrapped in silver and gold. A stone, deep blue and sparkling, even in the dim lighting.

The staff of the satyress.

The Mystic's staff.

The way to set the giants free.

Their way home.

It's-ending, it's-ending, it's-ending.

XXVIII.

Home. Home is very important. There should be nowhere safer than home. I wonder why the giants made their home unsafe. I hope they have learned better.

I clutch the staff in my hands. It doesn't feel very powerful. I look at Wink. Her mouth is wide open. "Painting," she says. "That's a painting."

I try to hand it to her, but she shakes her head. "You're the brave and fearless leader," she says, eyes bright. I laugh, a little, then shove the staff at Ull. He jumps back as though I have tried to stab him. He doesn't say anything, he just shakes his head. Ull isn't a person to keep quiet. This is how I know he is serious.

I turn the staff over, inspecting it. It's beautiful, but I don't feel like it's very magical, or like I can do much with it. "Where's the spell? What am I supposed to do?" I ask.

Ull licks his lip. "Goodness, I don't know," he says. "Maybe the *Annals* will clear it up, though?"

We all sit on the ground as he pulls out the *Annals* for us to look through. He skims. I wonder how he knows he isn't missing it, he's flipping so quickly. Furthermore, he isn't even good at reading Runic.

He gets to the end.

There's silence.

"I didn't see it," he says. He looks up at me, raising his silver eyebrows very high on his forehead. "Maybe you just have to… do it."

While part of me knows what he means, I am too embarrassed to try. To stand there, and just try...Try to what? I couldn't possibly. I blush.

"Come on, Peri," Wink says, encouragingly. "Let's do this!" She rubs her hands on her legs, and I look at her fabulous pinkie fingernail. Blue. I have always thought of blue as a sad color, but I think of the sky. I wonder if it's a brave color.

The staff has a blue stone.

Maybe blue is a brave color.

I stand up, gripping the staff tightly. I squeeze it, and I squeeze my eyes shut. I think about the giants, and my parents, and the Trolls, and Ai and her people. Then, I wish. I wish to be brave. I wish to share the *better* things. To make the giants feel safe and loved and together again. *Return,* I wish, suddenly. *Return, return, return.*

Suddenly, I hear a loud *pop* and I feel myself flying backwards, the ground suddenly leaving me--or am I leaving the ground?

When I open my eyes, I am outside of the 'cave,' sitting in the grass. I see a huge, glowing circle taking up the whole back of the cave. Blue, green, and purple swirl together. A real, live portal. I stare at my hands, clenched tightly around the staff. I did that, but it doesn't feel like I did. It feels like it came from somewhere, someone, something else.

I remember Wink and Ull. I sit up straighter, glancing around for them. There they are--sitting just a foot or two away from me. They are rubbing their eyes and gazing at the portal in awe. Reverence.

Before I have time to wonder what will happen next, I feel it--
the breath of a giant. This time, however, it is a gasping, excited
breath. It's the way Wink breathes when she gets a new book, the
way I breathe when the phone rings. I look behind me.

There he is. Mr. Giant. And then, then there are more. So
many more. All of them. Some of them wave at us, and we wave
back. I look at Wink and Ull. They are smiling so, so widely. I can
feel myself smiling, too.

Mr. Giant reaches the 'cave' mouth first. He turns and looks
at me before he enters. "Thank you, little one," he says, in a voice
deeper and stranger and more beautiful than any other voice I have
ever heard. "Thank you," he repeats, looking at Wink and Ull.

"I love you," I whisper. Then, I realize, "I'll miss you."

He just winks one of his huge orange eyes--not sad now, but
shining brightly. Then he turns and enters. In a blink, he is gone.
The others follow, laughing and cheering and hugging each other. I
feel tears prickle the backs of my eyes as I draw my knees up close
to me, watching them all disappear so quickly after they squeeze
between the rock walls.

When the last one has disappeared, an odd sort of energy
hangs in the air. I move closer to Wink and Ull. "Did you see that?" I
whisper. "I didn't dream it?"

Ull giggles breathily. Wink squeezes me in a big hug. That's
how I know I'm not dreaming.

I feel something poking my side, and I look down. There is
Ai. She has brushed her hair out, and tucked a flower behind her
ear. "Thank you," she tells us.

"Lovely hair," Wink says. Ull and I nod in agreement.

Ai blushes. "It's how he always liked it," she mumbles.

I'm beginning to guess whom *he* may be. I smile at her. "Whatever happens," I say, "you're beautiful and brave."

"You as well," she tells me. Then she looks over her shoulder and chirps a tree frog chirp.

A whole legion of brownies comes running up the slope now, some of them cheering. I look at Ai. "They wanted to come?" I ask.

She shrugs. "Many, yes," she says. "Others come for loyalty. They will come to love home," she says.

I hear Ull whimper when she says this, and I know that he will not view the magic world as home. He doubts Ai's words.

"Home, after all," she says, "is what you let and make it be." Then she turns to the portal, pointing straight ahead. "Forward," she cries, with intensity reverberating through her tiny voice. Her people cry out, too, a unified sound. Then they all rush in one moving mass, and suddenly--suddenly, they are gone too.

It is quiet for a long time after that. The sun is starting to go down.

"I really wish I could stay here," Ull murmurs. "I love it here. I wanted to learn more about everything here. I always thought I had so, so much time."

Wink and I watch him. He shivers, a bit, curling up tightly. "We'll be the next to go, you know," he says. "My parents will be here any minute."

"We'll visit you!" I tell him. He sniffles.

"Yeah," he says. "That will be wonderful." He smiles, a wobbly-tired smile. "You guys are the best."

"You're the best," Wink says. I agree. He blushes a silvery blush.

"Write so many good songs," I tell him. He grins.

"This is the ballad of Peri and Wink," he begins. "Not quite the story that one might think."

"That's lovely, son," a voice interrupts behind us. It's Mr. Troll. Ull stops and stands up.

Wink and I stand up, too. "Hello, Mr. Troll," I say, clutching the staff awkwardly.

He grins. Mrs. Troll comes up now and stands for a moment before walking closer to us. "Well done," she says. "So, so well done."

Mr. Troll looks at Ull. "Alright," he says. "Say your good-byes. The portal will close soon."

Ull turns to us. "Goodbye," he says. "Until you can visit."

Mr. Troll makes a strangling noise and glances at his wife. She is suddenly misty-eyed. "I'm so, so sorry," she says. "I didn't realize you thought... Darling, portals are only opened in times of great need now. Things have changed since the old days. Humans rarely come into our world unless they really must."

Ull has paled, a near-white silver. "No," he says. "Mother, no." He looks at me and Wink, then back at his parents. "Why? Peri and Wink *have* to visit."

His father shakes his head. "After humans began using smuggled magic and knowledge from our world for evil, the portals were closed. That was shortly before the Giants' War." He eyes the *Annals*. "You did read about the War?"

"Why didn't you tell me about the War?" Ull demands, balling up his fists.

"Some things," his mother says, gently, "some things we didn't want to bring here with us. Others, we just thought you'd never need to know. Not really. We scarcely believed..." her eyes look towards the portal. "It's closing," she says. "I'm sorry, we must go now."

Ull turns to us, eyes filled with tears. Then, suddenly, he kisses me on the forehead, then does the same to Wink. "Ullha," he says. "That means remember."

"Ullha, Ull," I say. "Ullha, Ull, forever." *Remember return.*

Wink says, "I'll paint you. I'll paint you so many times, with so many shades of silver."

He takes his mother's hand. "Ullha," he repeats. "Ullha, Peri. Ullha, Wink."

They head towards the portal.

We watch until they, also, disappear.

"I'll miss them," Wink says, softly. "I'd barely known them."

"The world had so much magic I didn't see. Then I did see it, and then it was gone."

She hugs me. I lean in and look at the ground. "Hey," I said, "Ull left the *Annals.*"

Wink stops hugging, for a moment, to pick the book up. "Huh," she says. "I wonder if he meant to do that."

"And I still have the staff," I say.

Wink nods. "I still have my key."

I realize that I left my key with the trunk. And that those things disappeared when the portal appeared. "My key is gone," I say.

"That's okay," she says. "You can come to my house and look at mine any time you want to remember. And I'll paint pictures of them."

Home. That's when I remember. "We were supposed to be home long before now," I say.

Wink's eyes grow wide. "Mom will be so worried."

We look back at the portal. "Will it burn out on its own," I ask, "or do you think there's something I'm supposed to--"

Boom.

It closes with a major explosion. Wink and I are knocked backward. I barely realize what is happening before I hit the ground and everything goes dark.

It's dark.

It's so, so dark.

I think I hear snippets of words in languages I can't understand. They're beautiful words, but mysterious. Maybe a little bit dangerous.

Then, suddenly, I am opening my eyes. My body is screaming as it rushes back to life.

And kneeling over me, staring at me with worried eyes, mascara running down her face, is my mom.

"Mama?" I ask as soon as I can speak. Is this more magic playing tricks on me?

It isn't. It isn't, because she throws her arms around me and squeezes so, so hard. "Peri," she gasps, "Peri, we were so worried."

She is here. She is real. She isn't a ghost.

I hear boots hitting the ground, running footsteps. My father. "Daddy?" I squeak. "How did you--but you were--"

"Oh, Peri-girl," he says in relief.

I peer over Mama's shoulder. The staff is lying there on the ground. No one seems to have noticed it. Wink's parents are hugging her tightly, as well, not too far away. She makes eye contact with me, then nods a bit, jerking her head to the right. I follow the movement with my eyes. There lie the *Annals,* as unnoticed as the giant magical staff.

We will not mention these. We will leave them and come back for them soon. They will be safe here until we can come for them. Sometimes, we both just know things.

It's-ending, it's-ending.

How can it still be ending, I wonder, when it is clearly over?

My mother loosens her grip, a bit. "We were preparing to come home when Linda called," she says, referring to Wink's mother, Mrs. McCall. "We made so many calls to get an express flight, you can't imagine." She squeezes me again, then starts crying harder.

"We were so worried," Daddy says.

"Mama, you must be so tired," I murmur, realizing, again, just how tired *I* am. "The jet lag."

Daddy laughs, but looks a bit pained. "Peri-girl," he says, *"you* must be so tired. We're going home now."

Home.

I wonder if I am ready to go home.

Mama squeezes me again. "You must be hungry, too," she says. "My poor girl. You're safe now."

I was safe the whole time. That's what I wish I could tell her. But I don't know how I would explain, so I don't. I just know that I am definitely ready to go home, especially with Mama and Daddy.

"I missed you guys a lot," I say, quietly. Then I close my eyes because now it is too hard to keep them open. "A lot."

I don't know if I dream this, or if I really hear it--Mama says, *we are so sorry, Peri-love.*

Finally, as I drift off in Daddy's arms, I think, *we saved the giants.*

And I feel like one of the lightest, heaviest things.

Epilogue

It's been about a week since we returned the giants to their homeland. I haven't seen Wink since, but today I am going to her house. She called yesterday to tell me she sent one of her older brothers for the staff and the *Annals of the Satyress*. He didn't ask questions. He didn't seem interested. I like to think that was the magic protecting itself.

I haven't had much of a chance to think about the giants, but I do miss them. I miss them in the quiet moments at night after Mama and Daddy have tucked me in. I'm actually feeling too old to be tucked in, but I don't tell them that. They haven't been around. They wouldn't know.

I'll lie there snuggled under my blankets, and I'll wonder--are the giants discovering things about each other now that they can be together again? I wonder if they're dancing, singing. I wonder if Ull has written any songs for them. Then I miss Ull, and I miss him so much that it almost overshadows the impressiveness of what we've accomplished, and the joy of having my parents here, with me, making up for lost time.

Not quite, though. Not quite.

I'm walking to Wink's, but she meets me on the tractor. "Come on," she says. "Come on, if we run, if we remember the way, we can make it there and back before anyone realizes we've gone."

I know what she means, and I know that we must do this. Sometimes, we both just know things.

She parks the tractor, turns it off, puts the key in her pocket. "With no pauses, detours, or tests this time, we can get there very quickly."

I take her hand--and notice that her pinkie nail is much shorter than it used to be. I raise my eyebrows. She looks sad. "It was very ragged," she says, softly. "But it'll grow back." She smiles. "I'll paint one of the keys on it soon," she says. "All gold. But the background, it'll be--"

"Silver," I finish with her.

She nods. She looks away. "Let's go," she says. "We don't have much time.

We start running, running north. The direction we've come to know so well. We run through the trees, through the pink-and-purple pines. They have remained, though they are rapidly fading in color. Soon, I believe, they will die. Maybe our world doesn't have enough magic to sustain them now.

Wink was right. An hour, tops, and we're there. We're standing there, where it all happened. And it looks so ordinary. A monolith, hollowed out. There is no trunk now. There aren't even any footprints of the giants, or the Trolls, or the brownies.

We stare at it for a moment.

"I don't know what I expected," Wink says. "Some sort of sign, I suppose."

"A sign of what?" I ask. We have proof that it happened, in the book, in the staff, in the keys. They are stashed away in the back of her family's old barn. They are safe. We have proof, in my parents' presence in my house. In all of the attention Wink's family has suddenly poured on her. Neither of us has discussed these changes, but I think we can see the benefits in each other.

"A sign of… something," she says, trailing off.

A slight breeze whispers past. It brushes against my neck, my shoulders.

That's when we hear it.

A snatch of song, as though from very far away.

Acknowledgments

So, movies get credits; songs get vague explanations at live shows; books get an extra chapterish thing called 'acknowledgments.' Welcome to the acknowledgments.

Through Him all things were made; without Him nothing was made that that has been made (John 1:3, NIV).

Without having a wonderfully accepting family, in which flights of fantasy, madness, and deteriorations into abstraction are encouraged, I myself would not be myself, and this story would not be itself. That said: Thank you, Mom, Dad, Maggie, Matthew, Ellie. I love you all. I wheelbarrow your will borrow. Especially I thank Mom, for comma removal. Thank you, Nanny, for all your help; especially helping me choose what name to publish under; I live in a constant state of existential crisis.

The story of this story began when, after an overly dramatic tooth extraction, I was confined to my house and forced to be still and quiet (can you imagine?). During this obnoxiously difficult time, Katie Grace gave me a writing prompt; That prompt led to the whole first chapter of this book. When the story elongated itself, she was there for it, encouraging it to surpass my intentions for its future. Thank you, KG, for being the greatest writing buddy anyone could wish. It'll be your story next---right? *Right?*

Next--to the Ulerichs. Mrs. Ulerich, this story wouldn't be what it is without you. It wouldn't be PUBLISHED without you. And, Anderson--thank you for the encouragement, and the Dish Domain conversations (let's have more!). To the rest of you, thank you for letting me into your house to ramble about made-up people. Not everyone encourages that sort of insanity.

Cody! We've survived the apocalypse, and we never even had to implement Double Tap! Thank you for all of the geeking out. You're the best 'adopted' brother.

Layna! If all of the times I texted you, 'so I have a new writing project,' were compiled, they would be twice as long as this book, and you know it. And yet, you've stuck around. That takes guts. LYLAS. I'm the real Slim Shady, and you know it.

Sof-Sof! Remember when we dabbled in fiction? And now... I'm dabbling in fiction? Where would I be without all of the experiments? Thank you very much.

To the magnificent being that is Clara--the letters! The phone calls! The obsessive messaging--and the *cover*. It's *gorgeous*. Thank you. And thank you for the excellent pen pal relationship. Here's to more madness to come!

Popsy, Jo--your kind words and critique of this book mean the world.

Aunt Annie!! (You get two exclamation points, did you notice?) The editing. Oh, my goodness, you did not have to do that, but you *did,* and *thank you so, so much.*

Chief Carrie, thank you for reading this when it was still a messy baby book with too many commas, and for the great discussions about themes and plot.

Of course, what would the acknowledgments be without mentioning BYONAP? To those of you reading this who don't know what BYONAP is, well, you can now live in a state of restless curiosity. You guys are the coolest. Ever.

To my blog readers--can I claim you as mine? Surely not, for you are all yourselves, and individuality is part of what we, the subpar artists, enjoy so much. You guys have been incredibly encouraging. Though someday I will look back at every single post and cringe and have sudden violent thoughts of throwing breakable things, I thank you all for your support. Subparity and clockhead man forever.

The certainty of forgetting someone who should not be forgotten is overshadowing every sentence here; nonetheless, this is where we are. Thank you, everyone! If you have been forgotten, then know that you weren't actually, because you fell under the blanket thank you. You are part of everyone, but not in a creepy *Ender's Game* buggers kind of way.

Good night Las Vegas.

About the Author

Photo credit M. P. Phillips, Jr.

Weez Phillips is a Christian homeschooled student living with her family in the Deep South. If you ask her how she's doing, she's likely to cry a bit and then spout contradicting statements before wandering off in search of fruit (nature's fast food).

CPSIA information can be obtained
at www.ICGtesting.com
Printed in the USA
LVHW090357290820
664466LV00008B/1430